# BIBLE STORIES
# FOR CHILDREN

For Elliott
Happy Easter!
From your Godfather

Tom

2019

# BIBLE STORIES
# FOR CHILDREN

Retold by Geoffrey Horn
and Arthur Cavanaugh

Illustrated by Arvis Stewart

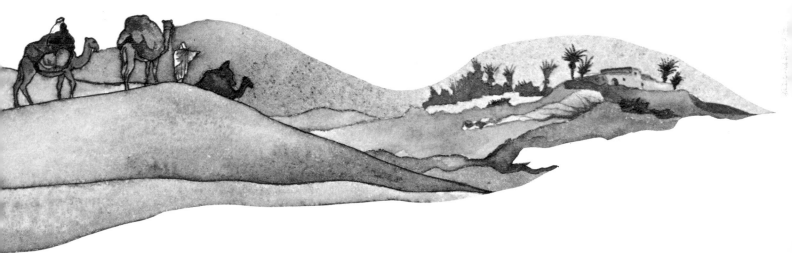

MACMILLAN PUBLISHING CO., INC.
New York

| | |
|---|---|
| **Editor** | Maron L. Waxman |
| **Art Director** | Zelda Haber |
| | |
| **Senior Editorial Assistant** | Susan Gootrad |
| **Assistant Art Director** | Trudy Veit |
| **Art Editor** | Marvin Friedman |

Macmillan Publishing Co., Inc.
866 Third Avenue, New York, N.Y. 10022
Collier Macmillan Canada, Ltd.

**Library of Congress Cataloging in Publication Data**

Horn, Geoffrey.
    Bible stories for children

    SUMMARY: Includes stories from both the Old and New Testaments.
    1. Bible stories, English. [1. Bible stories]
I. Cavanaugh, Arthur, joint author.  II. Stewart, Arvis L.  III. Title.
BS551.2.H648      220.9′505      79-27811
      ISBN 0-02-554060-2

First Printing 1980

Printed in the United States of America

# CONTENTS

# NEW TESTAMENT

# INTRODUCTION

**Bible Stories for Children** recounts some of the greatest and most inspiring stories ever known, stories that lie at the very root of our civilization. They have been told and retold, read and reread, for century after century. Parents have shared them with their children, and when the children grow up, they, in turn, pass them to their children. Thus, they have come down from generation to generation, an indelible part of our earliest memories.

The Bible is the sacred book of the Christian and Jewish religions, which first brought to the world the belief that there is only one God. In this greatest of all books, we see the struggles of our ancestors and their temptations as they lived among people who worshipped many gods. We see how they learned of God's greatness and love and came to understand the importance of his commands.

These stories contain the core of our religious and cultural traditions. They influence almost every aspect of our lives, from the way we think and the way we speak to the manner in which we view our fellowmen. To know these stories is to know much that is important about the history and the character of the Western world.

But for children a story is, first, a story. It must have excitement and meaning. It must be enjoyable to listen to, and it should create pictures that live in the child's imagination.

**Bible Stories for Children** offers a selection of the most important stories of the Bible. These have been chosen and recreated here for both their narrative power and their contribution to a basic understanding of what we believe and why we live as we do.

These stories are retold in traditional style, adhering closely to the flow and language of the biblical text. Such an approach gives the young child an authentic appreciation of the Bible. Your child will learn here just how Moses kept the children of Israel together in the wilderness; he will hear the words of the Sermon on the Mount as Jesus spoke them. The language and the stories have, of course, been simplified, but every effort has been made to retain the flavor of biblical narrative. Quotations from the traditional versions of the Bible have often been used so that the young child will become familiar with the language of the Bible and will be ready, in time, to read fuller and more complex versions.

Although the language is generally geared to the level of the young child, difficult words that are central to biblical literature are used when necessary. These are explained within the text, without interrupting the flow of the stories, so that the parent and young child can simply share these stories, especially when they are read aloud.

The illustrations are planned to underline and enrich the text. They are full of detail and recreate, with a rare vividness, the biblical scene — the desert with its harsh rocks and endless sands, the bustling towns and cities of the Holy Land, the crowds that followed Jesus' every step. These are pictures that will stay in the reader's mind throughout his life, to recall the power and strength of our religious heritage.

For the parent who wishes to expand on the stories as they are presented here, a Guide to the Stories is included, following this Introduction. It gives the book, chapters, and verses in the Bible for all the stories in this collection. Parents may, if they wish, consult the Guide before reading a story so that they will be able to put it into its full context. Older children may also find the Guide helpful when they begin reading the full Bible.

On every level, the Bible is truly the greatest book ever written and the greatest story ever told. It is the most important work of our religious heritage, in which we see the lives and examples of the men and women who have changed and inspired the world through all generations. **Bible Stories for Children** is intended to introduce young readers to the religious values, human drama, and richness of the Bible. We hope that sharing these stories with your child will be a spiritually rewarding and significant experience.

THE EDITORS

# GUIDE TO THE STORIES: Old Testament

## GUIDE TO THE STORIES: New Testament

The Old Testament

# The Creation

In the beginning, God created the heaven and the earth. The earth was shapeless and empty, and darkness covered the waters.

Then the Spirit of God passed over the waters, and God said, "Let there be light," and there was light. God saw that the light was good, and he separated the light from the darkness. The light God called day. He called the darkness night. *And so the first day of creation ended.*

On the second day God said, "Let the waters divide," and the waters divided. Now the world had two parts, upper and lower, with sky between. The upper part God called heaven. *And so the second day of creation ended.*

On the third day God said, "Let all the waters under heaven come together, and let dry land appear." God called the dry land earth, and the waters he called seas.

Then God said, "Let the earth bloom with fruits and flowers, and let each plant have seeds to make new plants." And from the earth grew trees with fruits, and grasses, and all kinds of vegetables. God looked at what he had made, and saw that it was good. *And so the third day of creation ended.*

On the fourth day God said, "Let there be lights in the sky to divide day from night, and to mark the changing seasons and the passing years." Then God made two great lights, the sun, to shine during the day, and the moon, to shine at night. These he set above the earth, among the stars and planets. God looked at what he had made, and saw that it was good. *And so the fourth day of creation ended.*

On the fifth day God said, "Let fish and birds fill the seas and sky." Then God created the great whales, and every creature that swims under water or flies in the air. God looked at what he had made, and saw that it was good. And he blessed all the creatures, saying, "Be fruitful and multiply." *And so the fifth day of creation ended.*

On the sixth day God said, "Let there be animals on the land." He made cattle, and wild beasts of every kind, and every creature that walks or creeps on the face of the earth. God looked at what he had made, and saw that it was good.

Then God said, "Now I will make a man and a woman, to rule over the fish in the sea, the birds of the air, the cattle and the wild beasts."

And God made man and woman in his image, after his own likeness. And he blessed them, saying, "Be fruitful and multiply. Be the masters of the earth, for I have given you food, and there is food for every creature on the earth." Then God looked at everything he had made, and saw that it was very good. *And so the sixth day of creation ended.*

This is how God made the world:

Light from darkness on the first day,

Heaven on the second day,

The seas, the earth, and green plants on the third day,

The sun, the moon, and the stars on the fourth day,

Fish and birds on the fifth day,

Man and woman and animals on the sixth day.

On the seventh day God finished his work.

And God blessed the seventh day, and made it holy, for on that day he rested.

# Adam and Eve

The first man God made we call Adam. God saw that the man needed a place to live, so he made for Adam a garden in Eden. In this garden he planted every flower that is lovely to look at, and every tree whose fruit is good to eat.

In the middle of the garden God planted a special tree. This tree had a fruit that was bitter and sweet at the same time, a fruit with a taste like no other.

And God said to Adam, "Of every tree in the garden you may eat as much as you want. But of this special tree you may not eat. For the day you eat the fruit of this tree, you will know about good and evil, and on that day you will die."

So Adam did as God told him. He lived peacefully in the garden of Eden, taking care of the trees and eating their fruit.

But he had no other living creature to help him.

Then God looked at Adam and saw that he was lonely.

"It is not good for Adam to be alone," God thought. "I will ask Adam which of all the creatures of the earth he would like for his helper."

God brought to Adam every beast of the field and forest, and every bird of the air. Adam looked at them one by one, and gave each of them a name, but found none to be his helper.

Then God thought, "I will make a woman for this man."

That night, God made Adam fall into a deep sleep. Then God took one of Adam's ribs, and from the rib he made a woman. When Adam woke up the next morning, the woman was beside him.

And Adam said, "This is my wife, Eve, who will help me and stay with me."

Together Adam and Eve lived in the garden. The days were sunny and the nights warm, so they wore no clothing. When they were hungry, Adam and Eve walked among the trees of Eden, picking the fruits that looked ripe and sweet.

But the fruit of one tree they did not touch. Adam warned Eve about this tree, just as God had warned Adam. And Eve too did as she was told.

Now in the garden there lived a serpent, a jealous beast. The happier Adam and Eve became, the more jealous the serpent felt.

One afternoon the serpent found Eve alone near the middle of the garden, where the tree with the forbidden fruit grew.

"You must be hungry," the serpent said. "Why not try this tree? Its fruit looks very sweet to me."

"God says we may take fruit from all the trees of the garden but this one," Eve answered. "On the day we eat the fruit of this tree, God says we will die."

"Die?" said the serpent. "Do you know what it means to die?"

"No," Eve answered. "Does it hurt?"

"God made you," said the serpent slyly. "Why would he want to hurt you? Surely you will not die."

Then the serpent saw Eve's confusion, and grew bolder.

"Listen to me. God knows that if you eat the fruit of this tree, your eyes will be opened, and you will be like him. Then you too will know about good and evil, and you will be as wise and powerful as God himself."

Eve remembered everything that Adam had told her about the fruit, and she remembered God's warning not to taste it. But the serpent's words also seemed to make sense. And she could see with her own eyes that the forbidden fruit looked as ripe and sweet as any in the garden.

Quickly she plucked the fruit from the tree and ate some of it. And when Adam came looking for her, she gave him some, and he tasted it, too. And so both Adam and Eve ate the fruit, while the serpent watched them.

When they had finished, Adam and Eve stared at each other.

Suddenly they felt cold and afraid, and covered their bodies with leaves.

Just then, God called out across Eden, "Adam!"

Adam, shivering next to Eve, said nothing, as they hid among the trees in the garden.

Again God called out, "Adam! Adam! Where are you?"

In a weak voice, Adam tried to answer. "I heard your words, O Lord, but I was afraid."

And God said, "Afraid? Why are you afraid? Have you eaten the fruit I told you not to eat?"

Adam answered, "The woman you made to be my wife — she gave me the fruit, and I ate it."

And God said to Eve, "What have you done?"

"The serpent tricked me, and I ate the fruit," Eve said.

Then all Eden shook with God's great anger.

To the serpent he said, "Because you have done this, I will make you the lowest of all the beasts. On your belly you shall crawl, now and always, and you shall eat dust all the days of your life." The serpent fell to the ground and slithered away.

To Eve he said, "Because you were fooled by the serpent, you will know pain and sorrow for the first time." Hearing this, Eve shuddered, and drew closer to Adam.

Then God spoke to Adam, saying, "Because you have disobeyed me and eaten the forbidden fruit, you shall work hard all day for your bread. The earth will be dry, tough, and full of weeds, and your body will ache from pulling them out. Nor will your work end until the day you are buried. For from dust I made you, and to dust you shall return."

To both Adam and Eve, God said, "Because you wanted to be like me, knowing both good and evil, you must leave this garden I made for you."

God made coats of animal skins to cover Adam and Eve and protect them, for bitter winds were blowing outside Eden.

Then God sent Adam and Eve out of the garden. Behind them he placed angels and a flaming sword that turned every way and blocked the path back to the garden forever. And so the first man and the first woman made their way into the world.

# Cain and Abel

Adam and Eve settled in a land east of Eden. There Adam worked the soil, bringing forth herbs and grain for them to eat.

Soon Eve gave birth to a boy, whom they called Cain. In time, Adam and Eve had a second son, whose name was Abel.

Now Abel grew up to be a shepherd. All day long he would follow his flock, letting his sheep graze through hills and meadows, and keeping them safe from harm. The family would often eat the meat he brought home, and Eve would make clothes and blankets from the soft lamb's wool.

Cain grew up to be a farmer like Adam. He worked in the fields from daybreak to nightfall, separating the green shoots and golden stalks from the sharp thorns and nettles that twined around them. When he came home at night, he was tired, and his hands were soiled and rough. Sometimes, wrapped in a sheepskin, he would lie awake in the moonlight, wondering why his father never complained about the hard work they did — much harder work, Cain thought, than the work of a shepherd.

15

Adam and Eve often thanked God for the two children he had given them. In Eden, they had spoken with God directly, but now they had a new way to show thanks. This was the sacrifice, a gift to God of something that was precious to them.

To offer their sacrifices, Adam and Eve built an altar of stones. On the altar they made a fire, and to this fire they brought their gifts for God. As the flames rose from the altar, they could see their gifts going up toward the heavens.

When the time came for the two brothers to make their own offerings to God, Abel laid on the altar a fat young lamb, the best of his flock. The flames leaped high, the fat crackled, and Abel knew that his gift was pleasing to God.

Then Cain brought to the altar the fruits of his harvest, grain and green herbs from the fields. Even as he knelt there, impatiently waiting for God to accept his gift, a steamy smoke choked off the flames.

Seeing that God had taken Abel's offering but not his own, Cain hardened his heart against his brother.

And God said to Cain, "Why are you so angry? And why do you look so sad? Know now that if you do well, your gift will be accepted. But if you do not do well, then evil lies waiting at the door. For though evil wishes to rule over you, you may yet be its master."

But God's words did not soften Cain's anger. Every time he thought of Abel's gift to God, hatred filled his heart like a raging fire.

One day, hiding his true feelings, Cain lured Abel to a lonely field, and there rose up against his brother and killed him.

And God cried out to Cain, "Where is Abel, your brother?"

"I do not know," Cain answered. "Am I my brother's keeper?"

And God knew that Cain had killed Abel and said to him, "What have you done? I can hear your brother's voice calling to me from the ground."

Then God cursed Cain, saying, "Now you

are more foul than the ground you stained with your brother's blood! No more shall you be a farmer, for the soil shall yield nothing to you. You shall become a homeless wanderer over the face of the earth."

Hearing this, Cain said, "O Lord, my crime is great, but the punishment is more than I can bear. You turn your face from me, and you force me to leave the land where I was born. Wherever I go, people will look at me and say, 'There goes Cain, an evil man, who killed his own brother. Let us kill him, too.'"

And the Lord heard Cain's plea, saying, "I will put a mark upon your forehead to let everyone know that whoever kills you, receives a punishment seven times worse than your punishment for killing Abel. This mark will protect you, but it will also remind you, wherever you go, of the great crime you committed."

And so Cain left the land of his birth, and settled in the land of Nod, east of Eden. There he lived and married and had a son named Enoch and bore God's mark on his forehead to the end of his days.

# Noah's Ark

God looked at the world he had made, and was unhappy. He saw that the people were acting in evil ways and had become mean and selfish. And their meanness had spread through the world like a sickness, poisoning all things on the earth. Earthquakes and volcanoes shook the land, for the earth itself was infected by evil.

God was sorry that he had made the world, and thought, "I shall destroy man, whom I created, and all the animals, and all the birds."

But there was one man who found favor in the eyes of the Lord. His name was Noah, the son of Lamech. Noah was the father of three sons, Shem, Ham, and Japheth. He was an honest man who followed God's way.

And God said to Noah, "I have decided to make a great flood that will destroy everything on the earth. Only you and your family will be saved."

Noah listened carefully to what God told him to do.

"Build an ark of wood, three hundred cubits long, fifty cubits wide, and thirty cubits high. Inside, make rooms, and take great care to seal all the cracks with pitch

so the water will not come through. The ark must have
three decks, with a window near the top and a door on the
side. When the flood waters cover the earth, this ark will
be a safe place for you and your wife, and your sons and
their wives.

"Bring into the ark two of each living creature, one male and one female — two of each bird, two of each beast, two of each creeping thing, to keep its kind alive. Then you must bring food for yourself and your family, and for all the animals."

Noah was a very old man, but he and his sons set to work as God had commanded.

When Noah's neighbors saw what he was doing, they laughed at him. When he talked of the great storm that was coming, they pointed to the cloudless blue sky. When Noah warned them that a great flood would cover the earth, they joked that they could use some water because their wells were running dry.

Even when Noah told them that God was planning to destroy the world because of the evil of men, his neighbors laughed.

After many months of hard work, the ark was finished. Then God said to Noah, "Go into the ark, and bring your family with you. And bring into the ark two of each animal and each bird and each reptile and enough food to keep them alive. For in seven days the rains will begin, and they will sweep off the earth all the creatures I made."

Noah did exactly as God commanded. And it came to pass that after seven days the skies darkened, and the waters of the great flood covered the earth.

Forty days and forty nights the rains fell. Water burst from the springs of the deep, and flooded through the windows of heaven.

For one hundred fifty days the flood waters rose, bearing the ark higher and higher. Water covered the hills and crested over the highest mountains.

There was water everywhere. Not a bird, not a beast, not a man or a woman, could be seen. God had wiped out all the living beings he had made. Only Noah and his family and the animals in the ark survived.

Then God remembered Noah, and sent a great wind over the waters. The waters began to drop, and the rains stopped. For one hundred fifty days the waters receded,

28

until the ark came to rest on the mountains of Ararat. Finally the tops of the mountains appeared. Noah waited forty more days before opening the window of the ark, and then he sent a raven from the ark. The raven flew around and around and could not find a place to land.

Then Noah sent a dove out. But the dove could not find a place to perch either, and it returned to the ark.

For seven more days Noah waited, and then he sent the dove out again. That evening the dove flew back to the ark with an olive branch in its beak. And so Noah knew that the waters were drying up.

Noah waited another seven days, and again sent the dove out. This time the dove did not return. Then Noah opened the ark and saw that the land had dried.

And God said to Noah, "Leave the ark with your wife and your sons and their wives, and all the animals and birds and reptiles. Build your homes again, and be fruitful and multiply."

Then Noah built an altar and made a great sacrifice to the Lord. And when God smelled the sweet smoke, he thought, "Never again shall I curse the earth in this way. Never again shall I destroy all the people and animals on it. Seedtime and harvest, cold and heat, summer and winter, day and night, all these will continue for as long as the earth remains."

And God blessed Noah and his family, saying, "Behold, I will make a promise to you, and to all who come after you, that I shall never again destroy all life with a flood.

"And as a sign of this promise, I shall set a rainbow in the clouds. So whenever a rain cloud passes and a rainbow appears, it will be a sign to me and to you, and to all who come after you, that I remember my promise and shall not send another flood."

# The Tower of Babel

The children of Noah had children, and their children had children. Though their numbers were many, all the people of the earth were still like one large family, speaking only one language.

These people did not stay in one place, but roamed through the desert. In time, they came to the valley of Shinar. Here they found clay and water to make bricks. They also found pitch for mortar, to join the bricks together.

"Let us build a city," they said. "And let us build a gigantic tower, a tower so tall that it will be famous for as long as men live on earth."

"How tall should we build it?" they wondered.

"Taller than the hills of Shinar," said one man.

"Higher than the mountains of Ararat," said a second.

"Why stop there?" said a third. "Let us build our tower all the way up to heaven!"

31

And so, with crude clay bricks and sticky black pitch, they set out to build their tower to heaven. Starting wide at the bottom, they built up and up in a great high spiral.

God was not pleased to see the tower rising out of Shinar. He said, "These people think they can build a tower to heaven and be just like God. If this is what people who speak one language think they can do, let the people speak many languages, and let them be scattered over the face of the earth."

No sooner had God spoken than confusion spread over the workmen like a thick cloud. If a workman asked for bricks, his helper gave him mortar. If he asked for mortar, his helper gave him bricks. Left and right, up and down, fast and slow — even the simplest words lost their meaning. Soon people were saying strange words with strange sounds, and no one understood anyone else.

The work stopped, and God scattered the people. Though we do not know who they were, we do remember the name of the famous tower they built. That tower is called Babel, for the confusing babble of languages that began there.

# ABRAHAM

God appeared to Abram and said, "Leave your country and your home, and go to a land I will show you."

Abram trusted God and left all he owned behind him. For many years he wandered in Canaan. There God came to him again. "I will make a solemn promise with you. You will now be called Abraham, for you will be the father of a great nation. I give this land to you and your children, through all generations, and I will be your God, for I know you will keep the ways of the Lord."

How could this promise come true? Abraham was an old man, and he and his wife, Sarah, had no children.

But one day, when Abraham was ninety-nine years old, God appeared to him and said, "Within a year, Sarah will have a baby boy, and you will call him Isaac."

Listening inside Abraham's tent, Sarah could not keep from laughing, for she knew that women of her age never had babies.

But God heard Sarah, and asked, "Why did Sarah laugh? Is anything too hard for the Lord?"

Then Sarah, fearing that God would be angry with her, pushed aside the tent flap and said, "I did not laugh."

"Yes, you did," God said, but he was not angry.

And it came to pass within a year that God remembered Sarah, and she gave birth to Isaac.

"Now I know why God made me laugh," said Sarah, cradling the baby in her arms. "It was so all the world could hear my laughter and share my joy."

Abraham and Sarah loved Isaac very much. Each day, they thanked God for their wonderful son, the precious gift he had given them. Even so, God decided to test Abraham's faith.

God tested Abraham in a way he had tested no other man. He said to Abraham, "You must take your son, your only son Isaac, whom you love, to the land of Moriah. There you must kill him and offer him as a sacrifice to the Lord."

Abraham heard what God said, and prepared to follow his command.

Early the next morning, before Sarah was awake, Abraham got up and saddled his donkey. Then, with Isaac and two young servants, he chopped the wood for the sacrificial fire, and they set out on their journey together.

For two days they traveled. The servants passed the time with jokes and chatter, but Abraham and Isaac said little.

On the third day, they reached a sheltered spot from which Abraham could see a mountain rising in the distance. He told the servants to wait while he and his son went on alone. Then Abraham and Isaac began the slow climb to the place that God had chosen for the sacrifice.

Isaac carried the wood, Abraham carried the knife.

They walked on in the morning stillness, until Isaac could no longer keep silent.

"Father?" he asked.

"Here I am, my son," said Abraham.

"Father, I have the wood, and you have the knife, but where is the lamb for the sacrifice?"

"My son," said Abraham, "God will provide a lamb for the sacrifice." And so they walked on together, saying nothing more.

When they reached the place for the sacrifice, they built an altar, Isaac handing Abraham the stones and Abraham fitting them into place. Then Abraham carefully laid the wood on the altar. Finally, Abraham took his son in his arms, and tied him with ropes, for this was the sacrifice that God had commanded. Isaac did not say a word as Abraham placed him on the altar.

Abraham picked up the knife and raised it above Isaac's neck.

Suddenly a voice called, "Abraham! Abraham!"

Abraham stopped. "Here I am!" he answered.

"Do not touch your son!" the voice ordered. "Do not hurt him in any way!"

At that moment, Abraham heard the bleating of a ram caught in a nearby thicket. Abraham took the animal and offered it as a sacrifice in place of his son.

Then the Lord said to Abraham, "Because you were willing to sacrifice your son, your only son Isaac, whom you love dearly, I shall bless you. And because you obeyed me and trusted me, your nation will have as many people as there are stars in the sky and grains of sand on the seashore."

After God spoke these words, Abraham and Isaac walked silently down the mountain and joined the servants in the sheltered place below. Together they made the long journey back to Beersheba.

# Isaac and Rebecca

Isaac grew up to be a strong young man. But before he was married and had a family of his own, Sarah, his mother, died, and Isaac fell into a deep sadness.

Abraham worried about his son. It was time for Isaac to get married, but Abraham did not want him to marry the daughter of a Canaanite. And so, after much thought, Abraham called his chief servant to him.

"I have an important job for you. Promise me that you will do exactly as I say," Abraham said to him.

"What is it, master?" the servant asked.

"You must go to the land where I was born," said Abraham. "There you must find a wife for my son who comes from the same family I do, and you must bring her back here to Canaan."

"I will, my lord," the servant said.
"But what if she will not come back to
Canaan with me?"

"God will help you," Abraham
answered.

The servant promised to do everything his
master ordered. Then he loaded Abraham's treasure
onto ten camels and set out on his journey to Haran,
Abraham's birthplace.

When the servant arrived at Haran, he stopped
near the well where the women of the town came to
fetch water every evening.

"Oh, God," he said, "help me. The women will
soon come to draw water from the well. Let me know

the wife you have chosen for Isaac in this way: When I ask a young woman for a drink, let the woman you have chosen answer, 'Drink, and here is water for your camels, too.' "

Soon a beautiful young woman came to the well. As she bent to fill her bucket, the servant ran up to her.

"Please may I have a drink from your pitcher?" he asked.

"Drink," she replied, "and here is water for your camels, too."

The servant thought that this was probably the wife God had chosen for Isaac, and gave her a gold ring and two gold bracelets.

"What is your name?" he asked.

"My name is Rebecca," she said, "and my father is Bethuel."

The servant knew that Bethuel was related to Abraham, and he thanked God for his help in finding a wife for Isaac.

"Is there room in your house to stay the night?" he asked.

Rebecca smiled. "We have plenty of food and straw for your camels, and a place for you to sleep."

At dinner, Abraham's servant explained why he had come to Haran. After he finished his story, he asked whether Rebecca would return to Canaan with him to be Isaac's wife.

Then Rebecca's brother and father said, "This is the Lord's work. Take Rebecca and go, and let her be the wife of your master's son."

In the morning, the servant came to Laban, Rebecca's brother, and said, "If Rebecca is ready, please send me back to my master."

But Laban looked doubtful. "Perhaps she should stay here a little longer," he said. "Ten days, maybe — and then she can go."

The servant spoke quickly. "This is the Lord's

work," he told Laban. "It should be done now. Send me home with Rebecca."

Then Laban called Rebecca and asked, "Will you go with this man?"

"Yes, I will go," answered Rebecca.

With this, Rebecca's family blessed her, and sent her on her way. Abraham's servant led the caravan, followed by Rebecca.

Now it happened that, as the caravan neared Canaan, Isaac was walking in the fields. He could see the caravan approaching, and Rebecca saw him.

Seeing the handsome young man, Rebecca asked, "Who is that?"

The servant answered that this was Isaac, who would be her husband. So Rebecca covered her face, for 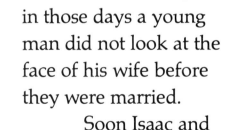 in those days a young man did not look at the face of his wife before they were married.

Soon Isaac and Rebecca were married, and Isaac took Rebecca to live in the tent that had belonged to his mother. And Isaac loved Rebecca very much and was comforted after his mother's death.

# JACOB AND ESAU

Isaac and Rebecca lived together happily. They prayed to God that they would have children, but not until Isaac was sixty years old were their prayers answered.

When Rebecca felt life growing inside her, she also felt fighting and kicking, as if a terrible struggle were going on inside her womb. "Why is this happening?" she asked God, for the pain was very great.

Then God said to her, "Two nations are in your womb, and two separate peoples will be born from your body. One will be stronger than the other, and the firstborn child will serve the younger."

In time, Rebecca gave birth to twin boys. The firstborn, Esau, was all red and hairy. The second, named Jacob, was hairless and pink, and was born holding Esau's heel in his hand. As the firstborn son, Esau was to become head of the household after Isaac's death. This was Esau's birthright, and it made Isaac glad, because Esau was his favorite.

Esau grew up to become a fine hunter and always brought fresh meat for his father's dinner. Jacob, though, stayed home most of the time to help his mother, who loved him best.

One day, Esau came home from hunting early, just as Jacob was cooking pottage, a thick bean soup. Esau had caught nothing that morning, and was very tired. The smell of the soup made him feel so hungry he thought he would die.

"Give me some of your pottage," he cried. "I must have something to eat right away."

Jacob thought for a moment. "Give me your birthright," he said, "and I will give you food."

Esau was so exhausted he could think of nothing but the thick red pottage. "What good is my birthright to me if I die of hunger before I can use it? You can have it, only give me something to eat!"

"Swear to God first," said Jacob.

So Esau swore before God that he would give his birthright to Jacob. Only then did Jacob give his brother a bowl of pottage and a piece of bread.

Esau ate his lunch, and returned to the fields, never thinking how cheaply he had sold his precious birthright.

Many years later, when Isaac was very old and his eyes were dim, he said to Esau, "My son, I may die any day now. Please take your bow and arrow into the fields, and bring me some fresh meat. Then cook it the special way I like it, so I can eat it before I die, and give you my blessing."

47

Now Rebecca overheard Isaac as he spoke to
Esau. When Esau left, she told Jacob, her favorite son,
everything that Isaac had said. Then she said to Jacob,
"Listen carefully, and do exactly what I tell you. Kill two
young goats from our flock, and bring the meat and
skins to me. After I cook the meat the special way your

father likes, take it to him and he will bless you instead of your brother."

"But, mother," Jacob argued, "Esau is covered with hair, and I am not. Suppose my father touches me, and finds out who I really am. Then he will curse me instead of blessing me."

"The curse will be upon me," said Rebecca. "Just do as I tell you."

So Jacob killed the two goats, and brought the meat and skins to his mother. Quickly Rebecca cooked the special meat for Isaac and gave it to Jacob to serve to him. But first she dressed Jacob in Esau's clothes, and put the goatskins on his neck and hands so that he would feel hairy.

"Who are you?" asked Isaac, when Jacob brought him the meat.

Jacob answered, "I am Esau, your firstborn son, and I brought you the special meat you asked for. Eat it, father, and then give me your blessing."

"How did you get the meat so fast?" Isaac asked.

"The Lord brought it to me," answered Jacob.

Then Isaac said, "Come closer to me, so I can feel whether you are truly my son Esau." And Isaac touched Jacob's hands, which felt rough and hairy because of the skins Rebecca had put on them.

Isaac wondered at this. "The voice is Jacob's voice, but the hands are the hands of Esau," he said. "Are you really my beloved son Esau?"

And Jacob said, "I am."

Then Isaac ate the meat and blessed his son, saying, "Let all people serve you, and nations bow down to you, for you shall rule this household and be master over your brother."

Jacob had just left Isaac when Esau came back from his hunting. He prepared the special meat for his father and then went to him.

"Father," Esau said, "here is the meat I cooked for you. Eat it, so that you may give me your blessing."

"Who are you?" Isaac cried.

"What is the matter?" Esau asked. "I am Esau, your firstborn son."

And Isaac became very upset, and asked, "Then who was it that brought me meat, and I ate it all and blessed him?"

With a bitter cry, Esau begged, "Bless me, too, father."

Sorrowfully, Isaac said, "Your brother Jacob tricked me. I gave him the blessing I meant for you."

Then Esau became angry at Jacob, and said, "My brother was born with his hand on my heel, and twice he has made me stumble. First he took away my birthright, and now he has taken my blessing. Father, have you not saved a blessing for me, too?"

"I have already given Jacob power over you, and made him the head of this household," Isaac answered. "What can I give you?"

"Have you just one blessing?" asked Esau, and he wept. "Is there nothing at all for me?"

Then Isaac said, "All I can leave you is the fat of the land to live on, and the dew from the heavens above. My son, you must live by your sword, and serve your brother. But the time will come when Jacob is no longer your master."

And Esau hated Jacob, and said to himself, "My father will die someday, and when the time for his mourning is over, I will kill Jacob."

# JACOB'S LADDER

Rebecca saw how much Esau hated Jacob, and went to warn her younger son. "Leave here and go to my brother Laban's house in Haran," she said. "You can return when Esau has forgotten his anger." To Isaac she said that Jacob was leaving because she did not want him to stay and marry a Canaanite. So Isaac blessed Jacob and gave him instructions for the journey, and asked God to make Jacob the father of a great nation.

Jacob set out for Haran with a heavy heart, and traveled from daybreak to sundown. Then, because it was too dark to go any further, he settled down in a rocky place, using a few stones for a pillow. Jacob was so tired that he fell asleep immediately.

As he lay sleeping, Jacob had a wonderful dream. Before him he saw a ladder that rested on the ground and stretched all the way up to heaven. And angels were climbing up the ladder toward heaven and down the ladder to earth.

Then Jacob dreamed that God was standing right beside him, saying, "I am the God of your grandfather Abraham, and of your father Isaac. This land where you sleep will someday belong to you and your children, who will be like the dust of the earth, spreading to the west and to the east, to the north and to the south.

"And remember that wherever you may go and whatever may happen to you, I shall be with you, and shall help you. For I shall not leave you until I have done everything that I have promised to do."

Jacob woke up frightened. "Surely," he thought, "this place is the Lord's house, and I did not know it."

Sunrise was still hours away, but Jacob, trembling, slept no more. He piled up the stones he had used for a pillow, and poured holy oil over them to let all the world know that God had been there.

Then Jacob promised, "If God will be with me, and help me, and give me bread to eat and clothing to wear, and let me return in peace to my father's house, I shall follow the Lord faithfully to the end of my days."

# Leah and Rachel

Jacob continued on his journey to Haran. One day he met some shepherds. "Where are you from?" he asked.

"We are men of Haran," they answered.

"Do you know Laban?" asked Jacob.

"We do," said the men. "His daughter Rachel is coming now, to water the flocks."

Jacob was happy to see his cousin Rachel, and greeted her with a kiss. When he told her who he was, she ran to tell her father, and soon Laban came to greet his nephew and invite him to stay in his home.

Now Laban also had an older daughter, Leah. Leah was plain, but Rachel was a beautiful girl, slender and graceful. And Jacob loved her.

After Jacob had lived with his uncle a month, helping him run the household, Laban said to Jacob, "Even though you are part of our family, you should be paid for your work. What can I give you?"

So Jacob answered, "I shall work for you for seven years if I may marry your daughter Rachel."

"I would rather she married you than any other man," Laban said. "Stay here and work for me."

Jacob worked hard for his uncle, but the years seemed like days to him, because of his love for Rachel. When the seven years were over, Laban held a great feast to celebrate the wedding.

After sunset, Laban brought his daughter to Jacob's tent. Joyfully, Jacob embraced his new wife in the darkness of their wedding night. It was not until morning, when the sun came up, that he realized the woman sleeping next to him was Leah, not Rachel.

"What have you done to me?" Jacob asked Laban. "For seven years I have served you so I could marry Rachel. Why did you trick me?"

"In our country it is the custom that the oldest daughter must marry first," said Laban. "But if you work for me another seven years, you can also marry Rachel."

Jacob, who loved Rachel more than Leah, agreed. And so, for the next seven years, Jacob lived with his two wives, working for Laban. Seeing that Leah was unloved by Jacob, God blessed her with many fine children. But Rachel had no children until she and Jacob had been married a long time.

Now Jacob worked for Laban for twenty years and became a wealthy man, and because of Jacob's hard work, Laban became rich, too. But Laban's sons were jealous of Jacob, and Laban was not as pleased with him as he once was.

And so the Lord said to Jacob, "Return to the land of your birth, and I shall help you."

Knowing that his uncle would not willingly let him go but that God would help him, Jacob gathered his family and all he had, and fled from Haran without telling Laban. But three days later Laban learned that Jacob and his family were gone, and set out after them. Riding quickly, he soon reached the place where Jacob had pitched his tents.

"Why did you run away?" Laban asked. "You left like thieves, not even letting me kiss my own children good-bye."

"I was afraid you would take your daughters away from me," Jacob answered. "For twenty years I have worked for you, and turned over to you the fruits of my labor. But even now, if God were not with me, you would have sent me away empty-handed."

And Laban answered, "These are my children
and grandchildren, and all these flocks are mine. But
what can I do about that now? Come, let there be peace
between us, and we will each return to our homes."

So Jacob and Laban finally made peace and
broke bread together. Early the next morning, Laban
kissed his daughters and his grandchildren good-bye
and blessed them. Then he departed for Haran, and
Jacob set out for his home in Canaan.

# Jacob's Return

The closer Jacob got to Canaan, the more he worried that Esau might still be angry with him. And so, one night when he stopped by a stream, he sent messengers ahead to greet Esau and offer him friendship.

Soon the messengers returned to Jacob. "We saw your brother Esau, and gave him your message," they said, "and he is coming to meet you with four hundred men."

"Four hundred men!" thought Jacob. "He must be planning to kill my whole family."

So Jacob asked the Lord for help, saying, "God of Abraham and Isaac, you said you would be with me if I returned home. I know I do not deserve your mercy, Lord, but please protect me and my family from my brother." Then Jacob spent a restless night.

The next morning Jacob sent gifts to Esau to show his friendship, choosing the finest sheep, goats, camels, and cattle from his herds and flocks. After Jacob sent the gifts to Esau, he ordered Leah, Rachel, and their children and the rest of his servants and animals to the other side of the stream for safety. By nighttime, Jacob stood alone in the darkness.

Suddenly he felt two arms around him, grabbing his throat and pulling him down. Without

knowing who had attacked him or why, Jacob fought back with all his strength.

Throughout the night Jacob wrestled with the stranger, their arms and legs locked together. Each time Jacob felt his breath stop or his eyes closing, he forced himself to fight harder, for he knew that if he gave up, he would die. But the stranger never seemed to get tired, no matter how hard Jacob fought.

Finally, when the stranger saw that Jacob would not give up, he pulled at Jacob's hip, ripping the muscles of his thigh, and said to Jacob, "Let me go, for the dawn is breaking!"

"I will not let you go until you bless me," said Jacob.

"What is your name?" the stranger asked.

"Jacob," he answered.

Then the stranger relaxed his grip, and said, "I call you Israel, a fighter's name, because you have fought with God and men, and won the battle."

Loosening his hold on the stranger, Jacob asked, "What is your name?"

"Do not ask me," he said. Quickly he slipped out of Jacob's arms, and was gone.

"I have looked at God face to face, and I am still alive," thought Jacob, amazed that he had lived through the struggle.

Then Jacob saw that the sun had risen, and that Esau was coming toward him with four hundred men. Wearily Jacob stood up and brushed the dirt from his clothes. Bowing low seven times, Jacob limped forward to meet his brother.

But Esau ran to meet Jacob, and kissed him, and the two brothers wept in each other's arms.

"Who are all these people?" asked Esau.

"This is the family that God has graciously given me," Jacob answered. He introduced Leah and Rachel and all his children, and each came up to Esau, and bowed down before him.

Then Esau asked, "Why did you send me all those presents?"

"So that you would be friendly to me," said Jacob.

"Thank you," said Esau, "but I, too, have been blessed by God and have wives and children and many servants and animals."

"Esau," said Jacob, "seeing your face again is like seeing the face of God. If you are happy to see me, please take the presents I have sent you, and my blessing, for God has given me plenty."

So Esau accepted his brother's gifts and said to Jacob, "Let us travel together to my home, and live there as one family."

Jacob thanked his brother, but said he could not stay with him. Instead, he continued on his journey back to Canaan, the land that God had promised to Abraham and Isaac as the place where the children of Israel would someday make their home.

# The Coat of Many Colors

Jacob lived in Canaan, and there raised his twelve sons. But of the twelve, Joseph was the one he loved best.

To show his great love for Joseph, Jacob made him a special coat. All the other brothers had coats of plain gray or white or brown, but Joseph's was a splendid coat of many colors.

Often Joseph would go with his brothers to tend the flocks, and sometimes he would come home and tell the bad things his brothers had done. Joseph's brothers hated him for this and also because he was Jacob's favorite. At times they could barely bring themselves to say a kind word to him.

Now one night Joseph had a dream, and the next day he told his brothers about it. "We were tying bundles of grain in the fields," he said. "Then my bundle stood up, and all your bundles made a circle around mine, and bowed down to it."

"Do you think this means you will rule over us?" asked his brothers, and they hated Joseph even more for telling them the dream.

Soon Joseph had another dream.

"Listen to my dream," Joseph said to his father and brothers. "The sun, the moon, and eleven stars bowed down before me."

When they heard this dream, his brothers were furious, and even his father was unhappy. "What kind of foolishness is this?" Jacob asked angrily. "Do you really believe your mother and I and your brothers will bow down before you?"

One day, Jacob said to Joseph, "Your brothers are out feeding the flocks. Go to them, and let me know how they are doing."

Joseph, wearing his special coat, set out to find his brothers. But when they saw him coming, they began plotting against him.

"Look," said one, "the dreamer is coming."

"Let us kill him," said another. "We can throw his body into that deep pit, and tell father a wild beast ate him. That will be the end of his dreams."

But Reuben, the oldest, stopped them. "Do not kill him," he said. "Throw him into the pit if you want — but do not harm him." Then Reuben hurried away, planning to come back later and rescue Joseph from the pit.

The brothers listened to Reuben and decided not to kill Joseph. When Joseph finally arrived and greeted them, they jumped on him, ripped off his wonderful coat, and threw him into the pit.

Then the brothers sat down to eat lunch.

While they sat eating, they noticed a caravan in the distance with goods bound for Egypt. Suddenly Judah had an idea. "What good does it do us if we leave Joseph in this pit?" he asked. "After all, he is our brother. Maybe we can sell him as a slave."

And so, when the next caravan for Egypt

passed, the brothers dragged Joseph out of the pit, and sold him for twenty pieces of silver. Then they all headed home without Reuben.

Soon after, Reuben returned to the pit. To his great horror, the pit was empty, and Joseph was not there. Filled with grief, Reuben tore his clothes. "Joseph is gone," he cried to his brothers when he caught up with them. "How can I go home and face our father?"

The brothers were ashamed and afraid to tell their father the truth, so they decided to make up a story to tell Jacob.

They killed a young goat from Jacob's flocks and dipped Joseph's many-colored coat in the blood. Then they brought the bloodstained coat to Jacob, saying, "We found this coat. Do you know whether it is Joseph's?"

"Oh, my son! My son!" Jacob cried. "Nobody had a coat as fine as Joseph's. Some terrible beast must have ripped him to pieces and eaten him!"

Jacob tore his clothes and mourned for many days. No one could comfort him in any way. "There is no happiness for me if Joseph is dead," he wept. "I shall miss him until the day I die."

# PHARAOH'S DREAMS

After Joseph's brothers sold him to the caravan, he was taken to Egypt. He lived there for many years and became a trusted servant to an Egyptian official named Potiphar. But Potiphar's wife became angry with Joseph, and told lies about him to her husband, who sent Joseph to the royal prison.

And it came to pass that one day, while Joseph was in prison, the royal butler and baker offended Pharaoh, the Egyptian king, and he sent them to the same prison. Joseph was told to take care of them.

One morning, when Joseph brought them their breakfast, both the butler and baker looked troubled. "Why do you look so sad?" asked Joseph.

"Last night we had strange dreams," they said, "and no one can tell us what they mean."

"Surely God knows what they mean," answered Joseph. "With his help, maybe I can explain the dreams to you."

The butler spoke first. "I saw a vine with three branches," he said. "First the vine had buds, then suddenly it had blossoms, and then ripe grapes. The next thing I knew, Pharaoh's cup was in my hand. I pressed the ripe grapes into Pharaoh's cup, and handed it to him."

Then Joseph answered, "This is what your dream means. The three branches are three days. In three days, Pharaoh will send for you, and you will be his butler again, just as before. When that happens, I hope you will remember me, and mention me to Pharaoh. For I am a Hebrew who was sold into Egypt, and have done nothing wrong. I do not deserve to be in this prison."

Joseph's words were so pleasing to the butler that the chief baker could not wait to tell Joseph about his dream, too.

"I dreamed I was carrying three white baskets on my head," he said. "In the top basket were all kinds of breads and cakes that I had baked for Pharaoh, but the birds were eating them."

Then Joseph answered, "The three baskets are three days. In three days Pharaoh will have your head cut off and hung from a high tree for all the birds to peck at."

And it came to pass on the third day, which was Pharaoh's birthday, that the king of Egypt freed the butler, as Joseph had said he would, and ordered the death of the chief baker, as Joseph also had predicted. But the butler forgot about Joseph, and did not mention him to Pharaoh.

Two full years passed. Then Pharaoh began to have strange dreams. They troubled him, and he called the wisest men in Egypt to tell him what they meant, but none of the wise men could explain the dreams.

Then the butler remembered Joseph, and said to Pharaoh, "Once, when you were angry with me, you sent me to prison. There I met a young Hebrew slave who correctly told me the meaning of a dream I had."

"Send this slave to me immediately," commanded Pharaoh. Pharaoh's servants rushed to the prison. There they found Joseph, shaved him, gave him fresh clothes, and brought him to Pharaoh.

And Pharaoh said to Joseph, "I have dreamed a dream, and no one can explain it. But I have heard that you understand dreams, and can tell their meaning."

"Not by myself," replied Joseph. "God will give you your answer."

So Pharaoh told Joseph all he had dreamed. "In my first dream," he said, "I was standing by a riverbank. And I saw seven fat cows come out of the water, followed by seven thin ones. While I watched, the seven thin and sickly cows ate the seven fat and healthy ones. That was the end of my first dream.

"In my second dream, I saw seven ears of ripe corn growing on a single stalk. Behind it grew another stalk, with seven ugly and misshapen ears. And the

seven badly formed ears swallowed up the seven ripe ones. I told all this to the wise men, but they could not explain the dreams to me."

Then Joseph answered, "Both these dreams have the same meaning, for God has twice shown you what he is going to do. The seven fat cows and the seven ripe ears of corn — these are seven good harvests. The seven sick cows and the seven ugly ears of corn — these are seven bad harvests, when many people will die for lack of food.

"Now, therefore, find a good and honest man, and give him the power to provide for the seven bad years. Let him save some of the corn from each of the good harvests, and store it in the cities. Then, when the poor harvests come, your people will have food to eat, though people in other lands may be starving."

Pharaoh thought this was a good idea, and told Joseph, "Since your God has shown you all this, you must be the wisest and most honest man in all the land. You shall live in my palace, and rule over my land. And everyone but Pharaoh shall bow down to you."

Then Pharaoh took a ring from his finger, and placed it on Joseph's hand. He also gave Joseph robes of fine linen, and placed a golden chain around his neck. Joseph rode in the chariot behind Pharaoh, and was ruler of all Egypt. And Pharaoh gave Joseph an Egyptian name, Zaphenath-Paneah.

Through the seven good harvests, Joseph gathered up corn, as much as he could, and saved it. And when the seven good years ended, there was famine everywhere, but in Egypt there was food.

# Joseph and his Brothers

The famine spread, and people came from all over
to buy corn from Joseph, the most powerful man in Egypt.
In Canaan, too, food was scarce, and Jacob called his sons to

him. "We must do something," he said. "I hear there is corn in Egypt. Go there, and buy some."

So ten of the brothers set out for Egypt, but Jacob kept Benjamin, his youngest son, home with him, because he was afraid something would happen to him.

When Joseph's brothers arrived in Egypt, they were brought before Joseph, who was seated in a fine chair and dressed in rich Egyptian robes. His brothers did not recognize him, but Joseph knew them at once. He made up his mind to test his brothers. "Where do you come from?" he asked angrily. "You must be spies who have come to Egypt to see what is going on here."

"No, my lord," they answered in fright. "We are honest men. We have come from Canaan only to buy food."

"I do not believe you," Joseph said. "You are spies."

But Joseph's brothers continued to protest. "We are twelve sons of one man in Canaan. Our youngest brother stayed at home with our father, and one of our brothers disappeared a long time ago."

"No, you are spies," answered Joseph, still pretending he did not know his brothers, and he sent them all to prison.

After three days, Joseph called his brothers before him. "Because I am a God-fearing man," he said, "I will give you a chance to prove you are telling the truth. Go, take the corn home with you, but one of you must stay in Egypt as my prisoner. He can return

to Canaan when the rest of you come back with your youngest brother. If you do this, you will not die."

Joseph's brothers were very unhappy, and they said to one another, "This is happening to us now because of what we did to Joseph. He called to us from the pit, and we did not answer him."

"I told you not to harm the boy," said Reuben, "but you would not listen to me. Now, after all these years, we are paying for what you did."

When Joseph heard these words, he turned away from his brothers and wept, for he, too, remembered what they had done to him. But Joseph did not let his brothers know he understood them. Instead, he chose Simeon from among them and had him tied up before their eyes. Then Joseph ordered his servants to fill his brothers' bags with corn, and also to hide in their bags the money they had used to pay for the corn.

When Joseph's brothers stopped for the night, they opened their bags and, to their horror, discovered the money. "What is God doing to us?" they asked.

As soon as they returned to Canaan, they told Jacob everything that had happened to them. Then they told him that they were supposed to bring Benjamin back to Egypt.

"No!" Jacob shouted. "Joseph is dead, and Simeon is gone. I will not let you take Benjamin away, too!"

But soon Jacob's family had eaten all the corn they had bought in Egypt, and Jacob called his sons to him once more. "Go to Egypt again," he said, "and buy more food."

Then Judah said to Jacob, "We cannot go back without Benjamin. But I promise you that if we return to Canaan without him, I will carry the blame forever."

"If this must be so, do it," Jacob said sadly. "I pray that God will grant you mercy and that you will come home with Benjamin and Simeon." And Jacob gave his sons rare sweets and spices as gifts for the great Egyptian.

When Joseph's brothers arrived in Egypt, and Joseph saw that Benjamin was with them, he told his chief servant to prepare lunch for them all in his own house. Joseph's brothers remembered the money they had found in their bags and tried to return it. But the servant said to them, "Do not be afraid. The money you found was a gift from God." Then the servant brought Simeon to them.

When Joseph came home, his brothers bowed down before him, and gave him the presents their father had sent from Canaan. "Is your father well?" Joseph asked them.

"Yes," they answered.

Next Joseph looked at Benjamin, and asked, "Is this the younger brother you told me about?"

When Joseph saw that it was Benjamin, he was filled with love for all his brothers and rushed to another room, where he wept alone. Then he went back to his brothers, and they all sat down to a happy meal. But Joseph still did not tell his brothers who he was.

When lunch was over, Joseph ordered his servant to fill his brothers' bags with as much grain as they could carry and again to hide money in them. Joseph also told his servant to hide his own silver cup in Benjamin's bag.

As soon as his brothers left, Joseph sent his servant after them. "Why have you paid back good with evil?" the servant asked when he caught up with them. "You ate my master's food, took his grain, and then stole his silver cup!"

"God forbid that we steal anything from your master," the brothers answered. "We tried to give back the money we found in our bags before. We were honest then;

why would we be thieves now? Please, search our bags. If
you find the cup in anyone's bag, the owner of that bag
shall die, and the rest of us will be your master's slaves.''

So the brothers threw their bags to the ground, and
Joseph's servant pretended to search them. When he pulled
the cup from Benjamin's bag, the brothers cried out and
tore their clothes in sorrow. Terrified, they returned to
Joseph's house, and bowed down before him.

"My lord," said Judah, who had promised his father that no harm would come to Benjamin. "What can I say? This is God's punishment for something we did a long time ago. Now we are all your slaves, and our youngest brother, Benjamin, is at your mercy."

Joseph spoke slowly, "I am not a cruel man. The youngest one, the one who had my cup—he must stay here. The rest of you may go home in peace to your father."

Then Judah came closer to Joseph and said, "O my lord, please let me say a few words to you, and I beg you, do not be angry with me. Our father is an old man who especially loves his youngest son. He did not want to send Benjamin to Egypt with us because he was afraid something might happen to the boy. Now I fear that our father might die if we come home without Benjamin. My lord, I do not want to be the cause of my father's death. Please let Benjamin go home, and keep me in his place."

When he heard this, Joseph could no longer hold back his tears. "I am Joseph," he said.

His brothers were amazed, and could not speak.

"I am Joseph," he repeated. "Joseph, your brother, whom you sold into slavery. But do not be unhappy about that now, for it was God who sent me here to save your lives, and the lives of your children. If I had not been sent to Egypt, who would have warned Pharaoh and saved grain for the seven years of famine? So hurry back to my father, and tell him his son Joseph is alive and wants him to come to Egypt."

Then Joseph embraced his brother Benjamin, and his other brothers, and they all wept with happiness. And when Pharaoh learned that Joseph's brothers were with him, he offered them good land, and sent wagons to Canaan to move Jacob's household to Egypt.

When Jacob arrived, Joseph went out to greet him, and they embraced. "Now I can die in peace because I have seen you," said Jacob. But Jacob lived many more years and saw his family grow rich and powerful in Egypt.

# The Burning Bush

Years went by. Joseph and all his brothers died, but
their children had many children, and the Israelites —
as the children of Jacob were called — grew strong in
numbers and in power. After many more years passed, a
new Pharaoh came to rule over Egypt, who knew
nothing about Joseph. This Pharaoh worried that there
were too many Israelites in Egypt.

"The Israelites have grown too strong and too
many for us," he said. "If there were a war, they might
join our enemies and fight against us, and become the
rulers of our country." So the new Pharaoh made the
Israelites into slaves, and put strict taskmasters over
them. The Egyptian taskmasters ordered the Israelites to

make bricks and work in the fields and to build great cities for Pharaoh. But no matter how cruel the Egyptians were or how hard they made the Israelites work, the Israelites continued to grow in number.

Pharaoh then decided to kill all the boys that were born to the Israelites. "I command you," he told the Egyptians, "to throw every baby boy born to an Israelite into the Nile River."

Now it happened that an Israelite woman had a baby boy. Because she did not want him to be killed, she decided to hide him. But after three months, he began to move around and make too much noise. So his mother made a large basket out of bulrushes, and sealed

it carefully. Gently, she laid the baby in it, put the basket at the edge of the Nile, and told her daughter, Miriam, to watch from a distance to see what happened to the baby.

That day Pharaoh's daughter came to the river to bathe. As the princess washed, she saw the basket in the rushes at the river's edge.

"Bring that basket to me," she told one of her servants.

When the princess looked into the basket, the startled baby began to cry. The princess felt sorry for him. "This must be an Israelite child," she said.

To cheer the baby up, the princess began to play with him. When Miriam saw this, she went up to the princess and asked, "Would you like me to find an Israelite woman to take care of the baby?"

"Yes," answered the princess.

So Miriam hurried back to her mother to tell her what had happened and to bring her to the princess. "Here is a woman who will take the baby away and care for him," Miriam told Pharaoh's daughter.

"Take good care of him," the princess said.

When the baby grew up and could walk and talk, his mother brought him back to the princess, who treated him like her son and called him Moses, because that name means he was drawn out of the water.

Although Moses was brought up in the Egyptian palace, he always knew that he was an Israelite. One day, when he was a young man, Moses went out to see how the

Egyptians treated his people. The first thing he saw was an Egyptian beating an Israelite worker. Sure that no one was watching, Moses killed the Egyptian, and buried his body in the sand.

The next day, when Moses went out walking, he saw one Israelite attack another. Quickly he pulled the two men apart. "Why did you hit him?" he asked the first man.

"Who gave you the right to tell us what to do?" the first man answered angrily. "Are you going to kill me the way you killed that Egyptian?"

Then Moses knew that someone had seen him, and he was afraid. "If this man knows," he thought, "Pharaoh must know." So Moses decided to leave Egypt and flee to the land of Midian. There he lived safely and peacefully as a shepherd for many years.

One day while he was tending his sheep, Moses came to a mountain called Horeb, a holy place. As Moses stood watching his flock, a bush suddenly burst into flames. The fire burned and burned, but the leaves stayed green. "I must find out why this bush does not burn up," said Moses.

When Moses came toward the bush, he heard a voice call from its midst, "Moses, Moses!"

And Moses said, "Here I am."

"Do not come any closer, and take off your shoes, for you are standing on holy ground," the voice said. "I am the God of your fathers, the God of Abraham, Isaac, and Jacob."

Moses covered his eyes, for he was afraid to look at God.

Then the Lord said, "I have seen the suffering of my people in Egypt. I have heard their cries, and I know their pain. I wish to set my people free, to lead them out of Egypt to a good land, a land of milk and honey — the land of Canaan. Come, I am sending you to Pharaoh, so you can lead my people out of Egypt."

"Who am I, O Lord, that I should lead the children of Israel out of Egypt?" Moses asked.

"I have chosen you, and I shall be with you," God answered.

"But what if the children of Israel do not believe me when I tell them that God has sent me?" said Moses. "What if they do not listen to me?"

"What are you holding in your hand?" God asked.

"A rod," Moses answered.

"Throw it down," God commanded. And as Moses threw it down, the rod became a hissing snake. Moses jumped away.

"Stretch out your hand, and take the snake by its tail," God ordered. As Moses grasped its tail, it became a rod again.

"If the Israelites do not believe you," God said, "show them this sign. If they still do not believe you, take a jug of water from the Nile, and empty it on the ground. The water will change to blood on the land, and then they will surely believe you."

"O Lord," said Moses, "I do not speak well. Sometimes I stutter, and my speech is slow."

Then God was angry at Moses. "Your brother Aaron speaks well. I will tell you what to say, and you will tell him what to say. He will speak for you in front of the people."

So Moses took up the rod that was his sign and left Midian to lead the children of Israel out of Egypt.

# Escape from Egypt

Moses and Aaron went to Egypt, as God had commanded, and came before Pharaoh. "The God of Israel says, 'Let my people go, so they can hold a feast for me in the wilderness,'" they told Pharaoh.

"I do not know who this God of yours is, or why I should obey him," answered Pharaoh. "The children of Israel are my slaves, and I will not let them go."

So Pharaoh sent Moses and Aaron away. That same day he ordered the Egyptian taskmasters to make the Israelites work harder. "From now on, do not give the Israelites the straw they use to make the bricks," Pharaoh said. "Let them gather the straw themselves, but do not give them any extra time to do it."

The work was impossible for the Israelites. They spent each day gathering straw and had no time left to make the bricks. But at the end of each day the Egyptians demanded the bricks, and beat the Israelites, telling them that they were just lazy. Confused and angry, the Israelites complained to Moses.

Moses had no answer for his people, and so he turned to God.

"Know that I am the Lord," God said, "and tell this to the Israelites: I have promised my people that I will free them from slavery and lead them to the land of Canaan. This I promised to Abraham, Isaac, and Jacob. The children of Israel will be my people, and I will be their God.

"I have hardened Pharaoh's heart so that I can show him that I am the Lord, who can do powerful things and who will lead my people out of Egypt with an outstretched arm. So go back to Pharaoh, and ask him again to let my people go."

Moses and Aaron returned to Pharaoh's palace. To show God's power, Aaron threw down his rod, and it became a snake. Pharaoh called in his magicians, and when they threw down their rods, they also became snakes. But to their surprise, Aaron's rod swallowed up their rods. As God promised, though, Pharaoh did not change his mind.

The next morning, when Pharaoh was standing by the river, God told Moses and Aaron to speak to him again, and again to show him the power of the God of Israel. Aaron lifted his rod over the River Nile, and struck the

waters with it. As Pharaoh and his servants stood watching, the waters turned to blood, and all the fish died. The river and all the waters of Egypt had an awful smell, and no one could drink for a week. But Pharaoh's magicians did the same trick, and Pharaoh would not change his mind. This was the first of ten plagues that God sent to the Egyptians.

Next God filled the land of Egypt with frogs — frogs in every stream, frogs in every house, frogs in every bed. Pharaoh's magicians made frogs, too, but no one could make them go away. So Pharaoh called Moses and Aaron to him and said, "Ask the Lord to take the frogs away, and I will let your people have their feast." But once the frogs were gone, Pharaoh broke his promise.

To show his power, God sent still more plagues to the Egyptians. The dust of the earth became lice, tiny insects that bit and stuck to all the people and animals. He sent flies that buzzed in the house of every Egyptian and every corner of Egypt, except where the Israelites lived. A terrible disease killed all the Egyptians' cattle and horses, camels and sheep, but the Israelites' animals did not get the disease, and they lived. One morning the Egyptians awoke to find themselves covered with boils, although the Israelites did not suffer from these painful sores. But Pharaoh's heart was still hardened against the Israelites. Each time Moses and Aaron asked him to let their people go, he answered no, just as God had planned.

So the Lord sent a violent hailstorm, with thunder and lightning, that destroyed everything in the fields, man and beast and all the plants. But where the Israelites lived, there was no storm.

After that, the Lord blackened the sky with locusts, great flying grasshoppers that ate all the crops and every green thing left by the hailstorm. But once the Lord answered Moses' prayer and blew the locusts into the Red Sea, Pharaoh refused to let the children of Israel go.

When, at God's command, Moses stretched out his hand the next time, a great darkness spread over Egypt for three days. No one could see anything or go anywhere, except where the Israelites lived. Then God said to Moses,

"I will send one more plague, and after that, Pharaoh will surely let you go. He will chase you out of Egypt."

So Moses warned of the tenth plague: "At midnight the Lord will pass through Egypt, and he will kill the oldest child of each family, from Pharaoh's son who sits next to him on the throne to the oldest child of the servant girl at the mill. A great cry of mourning will be heard all over Egypt. But among the Israelites, no one, not even a dog, will be harmed." With these angry words, Moses left Pharaoh.

To Moses and Aaron the Lord said, "On the tenth day of this month, every family of Israel should bring a perfect lamb to its house. On the evening of the fourteenth day, the lamb should be killed, and its blood smeared on the doorposts and above the door of the house. That night the lamb should be roasted and eaten in great haste, for it is the night of the Lord's Passover. On that night I will go through Egypt and kill all the firstborn children, but where I see blood, I will pass over the house, and the firstborn child will be saved. And you shall keep this feast of Passover forever, to remember how I brought you out of Egypt."

At midnight the Lord sent the tenth plague, killing the firstborn of every Egyptian family. A great cry went up, and while it was still dark, Pharaoh sent for Moses and Aaron. "Wake your people, and go, go all of you," ordered Pharaoh. The Egyptians hurried the Israelites along, for now they were terrified of the Lord and afraid they would all die.

To lead the Israelites out of Egypt, the Lord sent a great pillar of clouds by day and a great pillar of fire by night, so they would know the way.

After the Israelites left, the Lord again hardened Pharaoh's heart. "Why did we ever let the Israelites go? Who will work for us now?" Pharaoh wondered aloud, and he decided he would try to bring the Israelites back again. So Pharaoh chose his best soldiers and six hundred of his fastest chariots and set out after the Israelites. At the shores of the Red Sea, the Egyptian army caught up with them.

Seeing this great army, the Israelites were frightened. "Did you lead us out of Egypt so we could be killed in the wilderness?" they asked Moses. "We would rather be slaves in Egypt."

"Do not be afraid," he answered. "The Lord will save us." Then the Lord told Moses to lift his rod. All night long a great east wind blew the waters of the Red Sea apart, making a path of dry land from one shore to the other. The children of Israel walked through the sea on dry ground, with walls of water on either side of them.

When the Egyptians saw this, they chased after the Israelites, but in the morning, when they were halfway across the sea, the Lord looked through his pillar of clouds and fire and confused them. He broke the wheels off their chariots and scared the soldiers. "Let us turn back," the soldiers cried. "The Lord is fighting for the Israelites against us."

Just then the Lord told Moses to stretch his hand out over the sea. With a great roar, the sea crashed over the Egyptians and drowned Pharaoh's whole army, while the Israelites watched from dry land. Not one soldier remained.

In this way the Lord freed the children of Israel from slavery and led them out of Egypt. And they saw the great things the Lord had done for them, and gave thanks to him.

# In the Wilderness

After the Israelites crossed the Red Sea, they began a long and difficult journey through the wilderness to Canaan, the land that God had promised them. For the first three days they traveled without finding water, until finally they came to a place called Marah. Here they found water holes, but the water was so bitter they could not drink it.

"What will we drink now?" the people complained to Moses.

Moses turned to the Lord for help. God showed him a certain tree and told him to throw it into the water. Moses did what God told him, and the water became sweet.

At Marah the Lord laid down a rule, to test the children of Israel: "If you will obey me and do what I say is right and follow all my commands, I will never send to you any of the terrible things I sent to the Egyptians, for I am the Lord who protects you."

But the Israelites continued to complain. After their first month in the wilderness, they turned on Moses and Aaron again. "We would have been better off if the Lord had killed us in Egypt," they said. "There, at least, we had plenty of food to eat. You have led us into this wilderness to starve us to death."

Hearing this, God said to Moses, "The heavens will rain with bread, and every day the people will go out and gather as much as they need for that day. But on the sixth day, they should gather enough to last two days and save some of it for the seventh day. For the seventh day is the Sabbath, the day of rest, and on that day there will be no bread. These are my rules, and I will test the people to see whether they will follow them."

Moses and Aaron listened to God and told the Israelites, "This evening you will know it was the Lord who led you out of Egypt, for he has heard your complaints."

That evening, quails flew into the Israelites' camp, and the people ate them. The next morning, they were surprised to find the ground covered with something white.

"What is this?" asked the Israelites, when they ate the strange sweet food.

"This is the bread the Lord has given you," Moses answered. And the people said, "We will call it manna, because that means 'What is this thing?'"

Then Moses explained to the Israelites God's rules about how much manna to gather each day and how to save some for the Sabbath, the day of rest.

Most of the Israelites listened carefully to Moses' words, and gathered as much as they could eat in one day. But some gathered more and stored it overnight; the next day their manna was crawling with worms. And some did not gather their two portions on the sixth day, and when they went out on the seventh day, they found that no manna had fallen.

"How long will the people disobey my rules?" asked God. "I told them to rest on the seventh day." So the Israelites rested on the Sabbath.

In this way, the children of Israel learned to understand God's commands, and for forty years, while they lived in the wilderness, God sent manna to them.

# The Ten Commandments

On the first day of the third month after the children of Israel had left Egypt, they camped near the foot of Mount Sinai.

While the people waited below, Moses went by himself up the mountain, and God called to him, "Here is what you must tell the Israelites. They have seen what I did to the Egyptians, and they have seen how I lifted them out of slavery, as if they were carried on the wings of an eagle. Now, if they listen to me, and obey my rules, the Israelites will be my special people. They will be a holy nation."

When Moses came down from the mountain, he told the people of Israel what God had said. "We will do everything the Lord commands," the people promised.

God then said to Moses, "I wish to come before the people of Israel in a thick cloud, so they can hear me. Tell them to make themselves clean and holy and get themselves ready, for on the third day of this month I will come before them on Mount Sinai."

On the morning of the third day, there was a clap of thunder. Lightning flashed across the sky, and a thick cloud covered the mountaintop. Loud trumpets blasted. In the camp the Israelites trembled. Moses then led the people to the foot of the mountain to meet God. Mount Sinai was

smoking like a furnace, for God had come down to it in a
fire. The whole mountain shook. The trumpets blared
louder and longer. Then Moses spoke and God answered

him. Once again, God called Moses to the top of the mountain.

These were the words God spoke: "I am the Lord, your God, who brought you out of Egypt."

*You shall have no gods but me.*
*You shall make no statues or pictures of gods, nor*
*shall you pray to any god but me.*
*You shall not use the Lord's name in vain.*
*Remember the Sabbath day, and keep it holy.*
*Honor your mother and father.*
*You shall not commit murder.*
*You shall not commit adultery.*
*You shall not steal.*
*You shall not lie.*
*You shall not envy your neighbor or desire anything*
*that belongs to him.*

After God gave Moses these Ten Commandments, he told him the ways in which the Israelites should treat one another and all people with fairness and kindness. "If the people follow my rules, I will fight on their side against their enemies and give them long and rich lives."

When Moses came down from the mountaintop, he told the Israelites everything that God had told him. "All that God says, we will do," the people answered.

Then Moses wrote down all God's laws and built an altar at the foot of Mount Sinai. To this altar came all the young men, bringing oxen as gifts for the Lord.

Again Moses read all of God's laws and again the

Israelites told him that they would obey God's word. Then, as God commanded, Moses, with Aaron and the other wise men of Israel, went up the mountainside, and they saw God. He seemed to stand on a street of sapphires, bluer than the clearest sky. "Come up to me on the mountaintop, and stay there, so I can give you the stones on which I have written my laws," the Lord said to Moses. So Moses left the others behind, with Aaron to guide them, and went up to meet the Lord. To the Israelites below the glory of God blazed like a fire on top of Mount Sinai as Moses climbed up the mountain and disappeared into the clouds that covered it.

# The Golden Calf

For forty days and forty
nights Moses remained
on top of Mount Sinai.
When the Israelites saw
that he was gone for so long, they
became restless. "Where is Moses?" they asked
Aaron. Aaron tried to calm the people, but the longer Moses
was gone, the more impatient and afraid they became.

"We cannot be sure that Moses will ever come
back," they said. "Perhaps this God that Moses was going
to see is not the true God. Make us another god."

Aaron had no answer for the Israelites, so he had to
do what they asked. He went among the people and
collected their gold jewelry. This he melted down, and from
it made a golden calf. When the Israelites saw the calf, they

shouted, "This is our god that brought us out of Egypt!"

Then Aaron built an altar in front of the calf, and said, "Tomorrow we will have a great feast for the Lord."

The Israelites woke up early the next day and brought their offerings to the altar. Afterward, they sat down to eat and drink wine, and soon they were singing and dancing wildly.

When the Lord saw this, he was very angry. "Go down at once," he ordered Moses. "Your people have already broken my commandments. They have made a

golden calf and are praying to it, saying, 'This is our god who brought us out of Egypt!' I have watched these people and have seen that they are stubborn. Now I want to be alone so that I may destroy them. Then I will make a better nation from your children."

But Moses pleaded with the Lord. "If you destroy the children of Israel now, what will the Egyptians think? Pharaoh will say, 'Look, their God led them out of Egypt so he could destroy them in the desert.' Please, Lord, remember your promises to Abraham, Isaac, and Jacob, and do not destroy the people of Israel."

The Lord was moved by Moses' words and decided not to destroy the Israelites. Then Moses left him, carrying the two stones on which God had written the Ten Commandments.

As he hurried down the mountainside, Moses could hear the laughter and the singing grow louder. He came near the camp and smelled the smoke from the offerings and saw the people dancing wildly. Finally, in the center of their dance, he saw the idol of the golden calf.

Moses was so furious that he raised the stones that God had given him high above his head and smashed them to the ground. They broke into pieces. "How could you let the people do such a thing?" Moses asked Aaron.

"Do not be angry with me," Aaron answered. "You know how these people are. When you were away so long, they asked me to make a new god, and I had to do it."

Moses grabbed the golden calf and threw it into the fire, where it melted. He ground the metal into powder, mixed it with water, and made the people drink it.

Then Moses stood at the gate of the camp. "Let all who are on the Lord's side come to me," he called. To those who joined him, he said, "The God of Israel commands you to kill everyone who prayed to the golden calf, whether they are relatives or friends or neighbors." At the end of the day three thousand people lay dead.

Sadly, Moses spoke to the Israelites. "You have done a terrible thing, praying to a golden calf. Perhaps, though, if I go to the Lord and ask him, he will forgive you."

So Moses spoke with the Lord, and asked him to forgive the Israelites, and God agreed. Then the Lord told Moses to cut two stones like the ones he had smashed and to be ready the next morning to go up to Mount Sinai. Moses woke up early and took the two stones to the mountain. And the Lord came down in a cloud and stood with Moses, who bowed to the ground. "If I have pleased you, Lord," he said, "forgive my people, and make us your people."

"I will make a promise," said the Lord, "and lead your people to the land I promised to Abraham, Isaac, and Jacob, a land flowing with milk and honey. If your people will keep my commandments, I will perform miracles for them that have never been seen before. I will drive out the people who live in this land, and everyone will see these things and be amazed."

Moses stayed with the Lord forty more days and wrote the Ten Commandments on the two stones he had brought. Then he returned to the Israelites, carrying the stones, and his face shone with the glory of God.

# The Death of Moses

For forty years, Moses led the Israelites through the wilderness. These were difficult years, and the Israelites often complained about their hardships. One time in the wilderness of Zin, they came to Moses and once again said how foolish they had been to leave Egypt. "There is no food here," they grumbled. "There is not even any water."

So Moses and Aaron turned to the Lord. "The people are thirsty," they said. "What shall we tell them?"

"I will show you a rock in this wilderness," the Lord said. "Gather the Israelites there. When you speak to the rock, water will flow from it."

The people continued to complain as Moses and Aaron gathered them at the rock. Hearing their complaints, Moses lost his patience. "Listen to me, you ungrateful people," he shouted. "Must Aaron and I get you water from this rock?" And, without thinking, Moses twice slammed his rod against the rock. Water came rushing out, and the people drank.

But what Moses did angered the Lord. "I told you to speak to the rock, not to hit it," he said. "I wanted you to show the Israelites how much the Lord would do to help them, but in front of everyone, you disobeyed me and let your anger get the better of you. Because of this, you and Aaron will not lead the people into the land I promised you."

Soon after, Aaron died, and God chose his son Eleazar to be high priest in Aaron's place. The Israelites mourned Aaron's death for a month and then continued their journey. After a time, they left the wilderness of Zin and came close to the River Jordan. Across it lay Canaan, the land God had promised them.

Knowing he would die soon, Moses spoke to God. "Please Lord," he asked, "let the Israelites know who will lead them into Canaan, so they will not be like sheep who have lost their shepherd."

"Take Joshua, the son of Nun," the Lord answered, "and give him some of your power over the Israelites. In this way, the people will learn to obey him."

So Moses did what God commanded, and stood with Joshua before the high priest Eleazar, to show the Israelites that Joshua would lead them when Moses was no longer there.

When the Israelites were getting ready to cross the Jordan, Moses called them together and spoke to them for the last time. He talked about the forty hard years they had spent in the wilderness, and all the things that had happened to them. He reminded them to obey all of God's commandments, so that they would please God and be a great people. Moses then sang a song of thanks to God and blessed the Israelites, saying, "Happy are you, O Israel, a people saved by the Lord."

Then Moses went up to Mount Neboh. From the mountaintop the Lord showed Moses the whole of Canaan, from the walled city of Jericho all the way to the sea. This was the land, God said, that he had promised to Abraham, to Isaac, and to Jacob.

There, on Mount Neboh, Moses died, in his one hundred and twentieth year, still a strong man. Moses was a true servant of God, a man who had known God face to face and who had led the people of Israel out of Egypt.

# THE BATTLE OF JERICHO

After Moses died, God said to Joshua, "My servant Joshua, you must now lead the children of Israel into the land I promised them. I stood with Moses, and I will also stand by you. Be strong, have courage, and follow all my laws, and I will always be with you."

"Get ready," Joshua told the Israelites, "for in three days you will cross the Jordan River into the land that God has promised you."

Now Joshua knew that if the Israelites were to settle in the land of Canaan, they would have to fight the Canaanites who already lived there. To find out whether the Canaanites were getting ready to fight, Joshua sent two spies to Jericho. The spies crossed the Jordan and entered the walled city. There they stayed with a woman named Rahab. But some Canaanites saw the two strangers and told the king of Jericho. "Go to the house of Rahab and find those men," the king told his soldiers.

When the soldiers came to her house, Rahab told them, "Two men were here, but I had no idea who they were. At nightfall, they left. If you hurry to the city gate, perhaps you can catch up with them."

The soldiers rushed away. Meanwhile, the two spies were safe where Rahab had hidden them on the roof of her house.

"I know that the Lord has given you this land," she told the Israelite spies. "Everyone here is very frightened of you. We have heard how the Lord dried up the Red Sea for you and defeated the Egyptians. When we heard your people were coming, our hearts were filled with fear. All I ask," she continued, "is that when you destroy Jericho, you save my father, my mother, my brothers, and my sisters, as I have saved you."

"We promise," answered the men. Then Rahab let a red rope down from her window, which looked out over the city wall. The two spies climbed through the window and escaped from Jericho.

"Truly the Lord has given us this land," the spies told Joshua when they returned to camp. "Everyone in Jericho is afraid of us."

On hearing this news, Joshua ordered the Israelites to move their camp closer to the Jordan. "Tomorrow," Joshua said, "the Lord will work wonders."

The people were told to follow the priests, who would carry the Ark of the Covenant, the great gold-covered chest in which the Ten Commandments were kept. This was the Ark the Lord had commanded the Israelites to build at Mount Sinai.

The moment the first priest carrying the Ark set foot in the Jordan River, the waters stopped flowing, and the people crossed safely. Not until all the Israelites stood on the opposite bank did the waters of the river start to flow again. When Joshua came near Jericho, he looked up and saw a man standing with a sword in his hand. "Are you with us or against us?" Joshua asked.

"I am a captain in the armies of the Lord," the
soldier answered. Then God came to that holy place and
told Joshua how Jericho would be destroyed.

After Joshua explained God's plan to the people, the
Israelites marched once around the heavily guarded city.
First came the soldiers, in full battle dress, and next came
seven priests carrying the Ten Commandments and
trumpets made of rams' horns. On the second day they did
the same thing, and then for four more days. But on the
seventh day the army and the priests circled the city seven
times. Then the priests blew a long blast on their horns.

125

"Shout! Shout as loud as you can!" Joshua called to the Israelites. "The Lord has given you the city!"

So the people shouted, and when the sound of the horns and the mighty shout went thundering through the city, the great walls of Jericho trembled and came crashing down. The Israelites rushed into the city and destroyed it, saving only Rahab and her family. All the gold and silver the Israelites found in the city they offered to God, who had given them this great victory. Then they burned Jericho to the ground.

# GIDEON'S TRUMPETS

The Israelites finally conquered all of Canaan and lived there many years. But in time they began to act like the Canaanites and to pray to the gods of the Canaanites. This made the Lord angry, and he set the Midianites to rule over the Israelites for seven hard years.

One day, as a young Israelite named Gideon was working, a stranger suddenly appeared. "The Lord is with you," the stranger said.

"If the Lord is with us," asked Gideon, "why has all this happened? Why do we live in caves while the Midianites steal our grain and our cattle? Where are the miracles my father and grandfather talk about?"

"You will save Israel from the Midianites," answered the stranger.

"How can that be?" said Gideon. "My family is poor, and I am the youngest son."

"The Lord will be with you," said the stranger.

"If the Lord is with me, show me a sign," said Gideon.

The stranger waited while Gideon made him supper, then told him to put it on a rock. Reaching out his stick, the stranger touched the food. The rock burst into flames, burning the supper to ashes, and the stranger

disappeared. Then Gideon knew that the stranger was an angel of the Lord.

That night God told Gideon to destroy an altar to Baal, a Canaanite god, and build one to him in its place. The next morning, when the men of the town saw the new altar, they wanted to kill Gideon. But Gideon's father stopped them. "Will you defend Baal?" he shouted. "If Baal is a god, let him stand up for himself." The men walked slowly away.

Soon the Midianites and other neighboring tribes decided to destroy the Israelites. Gideon, filled with the Spirit of God, sounded his trumpet and called all Israel into battle. But as the days passed and the Midianites and the Israelites got ready for war, Gideon began to worry. "Please, Lord," Gideon said to God, "do not be angry with me. I must know for sure if I am to save Israel. If I am, show me more signs."

So God showed Gideon more signs, and Gideon believed the Lord. Then God said, "You have too many men in your army. If the Israelites win this battle with such a large army, they will think they won all by themselves, and not because I helped them. Tell everyone who is frightened to go home."

When Gideon told his soldiers this, twenty-two thousand men decided to go home, leaving an army of only ten thousand men. "You still have too many men," God said. "Take them down to the river, and I will pick the men who should go with you."

At the river, Gideon told his men to drink. Most of the soldiers knelt down and drank the water, but three hundred soldiers put their faces right into the river and lapped up the water like dogs. These were the men God chose for Gideon's army. Gideon sent the rest of the men home.

Then Gideon ordered each of his three hundred men to carry only an empty jar, a torch, and a trumpet for weapons. On the night of the battle, God told Gideon to go to the Midianite camp and listen to what the enemy soldiers were saying. "This will give you courage," he said.

When Gideon got near the camp, he saw thousands of Midianite soldiers getting ready for battle. He crept closer, and heard one of them telling his friend a bad dream. A loaf of barley bread had rolled into the Midianite camp, the soldier said, and it turned over his tent. "The bread is the sword of Gideon," answered his friend. "God has given him the victory."

Gideon hurried back to his camp. "Wake up, get ready!" he shouted. "The Lord has given us the battle."

Quietly Gideon's men surrounded the Midianite camp. When they were in place, Gideon blew his trumpet. At this signal, all the Israelites blew their trumpets, smashed their jars on the ground, and waved their torches madly. "A sword for the Lord and for Gideon!" they shouted.

The clattering of the pottery, the blare of the trumpets, and the flashing of the torch lights startled the Midianites. Terrified and half asleep, they began to run in all directions. They were so confused they attacked one another. By morning, the enemy camp was empty, and Israel's victory over Midian had begun.

# Samson and the Philistines

Now it happened that the Israelites again disobeyed the Lord, and he punished them by making the Philistines rule over them. At this time an angel appeared to an Israelite woman who had never been able to bear children. "You will soon have a son," he said, "and he will lead the fight to free the Israelites from the Philistines. But be sure that his hair is never cut, nor his beard shaved, for that is a sign that his life belongs to God."

The boy was born, and he was named Samson. Samson was a huge and powerful man, as brave as he was strong. Once, when a young lion threatened him, Samson ripped the animal to pieces with his bare hands. Some time later, he passed the dead body of the lion and saw bees buzzing round it. He reached inside the body, took the honey, and ate it all the way home.

Samson was always fighting with the Philistines. One time, a Philistine cheated Samson and made him angry. So Samson went out and caught three hundred foxes. He tied their tails together, two foxes at a time, and attached a burning torch to each pair of animals. The foxes ran through the fields of the Philistines, burning all their crops. Furious, the Philistines sent their soldiers to the Israelites. "Where is Samson?" they asked.

The Israelites went to a cave where they knew Samson was hiding. "You are making trouble for us," they said. "We are going to tie you up and give you to the Philistines."

When the Philistines saw Samson all tied up, they shouted with joy. But the Lord sent a great burst of strength to Samson. He tore off the ropes that bound him and picked up the jawbone of an ass from the ground. With that for a weapon, he killed a thousand Philistines. After Samson destroyed the Philistine army, he became the leader of the Israelite people.

Samson led the Israelites for twenty years. The Philistines made many plans to kill him, but never caught him. Finally, when Samson fell in love with a beautiful woman named

Delilah, the Philistine leaders saw their chance. "Find out what makes Samson so strong and how we can capture him," they told Delilah, "and we will give you eleven hundred pieces of silver."

Delilah gladly accepted the Philistines' offer.

"What is the secret of your strength?" she asked Samson one day.

"Tie me up with seven fresh bowstrings," Samson lied, "and I will be as weak as any man."

After Samson fell asleep, Delilah tied him with the bowstrings and shouted, "The Philistines are coming!" But Samson snapped the bowstrings as if they were threads.

"You have made a fool of me," Delilah said. "Now tell me how I can really tie you up."

"Try new ropes that have never been used before," said Samson.

So that night Delilah tied new ropes around Samson and again shouted, "The Philistines are coming!" But Samson popped the ropes as if they were dry vines.

"How can you say you love me when you lie to me and make a fool of me?" asked Delilah.

Day after day Delilah asked the same question until Samson finally lost his patience. "Here is my secret," he said angrily. "I have never shaved or cut my hair. If I shaved, I would lose all my strength."

Delilah knew she had Samson's secret at last. She sang softly to him and made him fall asleep with his head on her lap. Quickly she called for a barber, who cut off Samson's hair. This time, when Delilah shouted, "The Philistines are coming!" Samson could hardly move.

So the Philistines finally captured Samson, and they put out his eyes. Then they threw him into prison and made him grind corn, turning the great wheel at the mill like an animal.

Once in a while, the prison guards brought out the blind Samson so that the children could tease him and laugh at him. But all the time the guards never noticed that Samson's hair was growing back.

One day, the Philistines gathered in their temple to celebrate. "Bring out Samson," they shouted. And the Philistines laughed when they saw the blind Samson led into the temple. After a while, Samson said to the guards, "I feel tired. Could you lead me to the pillars that hold up the temple so I can rest against them?"

"O Lord," prayed Samson as he felt the pillars on both sides, "remember me, and make me strong this one last time, so I can pay the Philistines back for what they did to my eyes!"

Samson took hold of the two pillars, one with his right arm and the other with his left, and pulled forward with all his strength. "Let me die with the Philistines," shouted Samson as the roof of the temple fell in, killing everyone in the building. So in his death Samson killed more Philistines than he had in his lifetime.

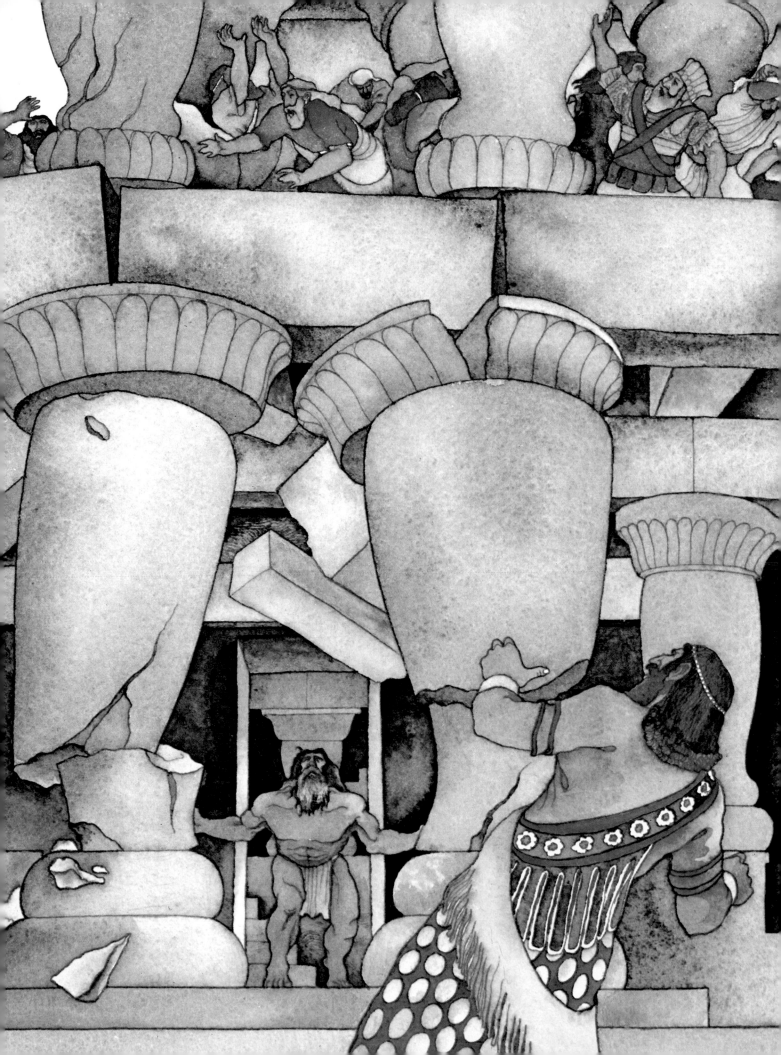

# Ruth and Naomi

There once was a famine in the land of the Israelites, and a young man named Elimelech, who lived near Bethlehem, went with his wife and two sons to Moab, where there was still enough food.

Shortly after the family settled in Moab, Elimelech died. His wife, Naomi, was left with her sons, who chose wives from among the Moabites. One of these women was named Orpah; the other was named Ruth. They all lived in Moab for about ten years. But then both sons died, leaving only Naomi and her two daughters by marriage.

Naomi's life had been hard, so when she heard that the famine in her homeland was over, she decided to leave Moab. Her daughters-in-law went part of the way with her, but as Naomi came near her homeland, she told them, "Now you must both go back to your mothers. May the Lord be kind to you, as you have been to me." Then the three women hugged each other and wept.

Sadly, Orpah left her mother-in-law, but Ruth clung to Naomi. "Orpah is going back to her home and the gods of her people," said Naomi. "You should do the same thing, Ruth, for you will be a stranger in my land."

"Do not ask me to leave you," Ruth begged. "Wherever you go, I will go, and wherever you live, I will live. Your people will be my people, and your God will be my God. Only death will part us."

When Naomi saw how much Ruth loved her, she did not argue with her any further. The two women went on together, until they reached Bethlehem, just as the barley harvest was beginning. In those days poor people used to follow the harvesters and glean, picking up any stalks of grain the workers left behind.

"I will go out and glean for our food," Ruth said.

Ruth first came to the fields of Boaz, an Israelite known for his kindness and generosity. Ruth did not know he came from the same family as Naomi's husband, Elimelech. After a few days Boaz noticed how hard Ruth was working, and asked who she was.

"She is the Moabite girl who came here with Naomi," the workers said.

Boaz went over to Ruth. "Do not glean in anyone else's fields," he told her kindly. "Keep close to the other women, so that the young men do not bother you. Take what you need, and when you are thirsty, drink the water that my young men have drawn from the well."

Ruth bowed low before him. "Why are you so kind to me?" she asked. "I am a stranger here."

"I have heard how you left your home to stay with Naomi," he said. "The Lord of Israel will reward you for it."

Then Boaz gave Ruth some food to eat, and told his field workers to let her glean whenever she wanted. He even told them to leave a few extra stalks for her to pick up.

Ruth stayed for the entire barley season, and for the wheat harvest that followed. Each morning Boaz watched her walk through his fields, taking only as much grain as she needed. Each night he watched her leave his fields and return to Naomi, bringing the grain for their bread. He saw how Ruth kept close to the other women, and did not waste time with the young men. The more Boaz saw Ruth, the more he liked her, and by the time the harvest was over, he decided to marry her. Naomi was delighted. "The Lord has watched over us and taken care of us," she said.

Soon after, Boaz and Ruth had a son named Obed, and Naomi loved her grandchild. When he was grown, Obed had a son named Jesse. Jesse was the father of David, and David became the greatest king the Israelites ever had.

# SAMUEL AND SAUL

For many years after the Israelites conquered Canaan, they had no kings. God had given the Israelites the Ten Commandments, and great men, who were called judges, led the people. But in time, the Israelites decided that they should have a king, like other nations. The people went to Samuel, who was then their judge. "Choose a king for us," they told him.

Not knowing how to answer them, Samuel asked the Lord what to do. "Listen to the people," the Lord said. "Let them have a king if they want one, since they no longer trust me to lead them. But first tell them what will happen if they have a king."

So Samuel warned the Israelites. "If you have a king," he told them, "he will take your sons and make them drive his chariots and plow his fields. He will take your daughters and make them his cooks and bakers. Then he will take the best of your crops and your wine and your animals and use them to feed his household. Finally you will become his slaves. When that happens, you will call out to the Lord to help you, but he will not listen to you."

The Israelites would not believe Samuel. "We still want a king," they said. Now God had told Samuel to do

whatever the people wanted, so he chose a man named
Saul to be the first king of Israel.

Saul was a brave and handsome man who stood a
full head taller than anyone else. God had picked him to
save the Israelites from the Philistines, and he fought many
battles and won many victories. One day, Samuel came to
Saul and said to him, "The Lord remembers how once the
Amalekites attacked the Israelites when they came out of
Egypt, and now he wants to punish them. He orders you to
destroy everything in the city of Amalek — men, women,

children, even camels, oxen, and sheep. No living thing is to be spared."

So Saul raised a powerful army and marched on Amalek. He destroyed it entirely, sparing only Agag, the king of the Amalekites. The soldiers slaughtered all the thin and sickly animals in the city but did not kill the plump lambs and healthy calves.

"I am sorry I made Saul king," the Lord told Samuel after the battle. "He has not followed my commands."

The next morning Samuel woke up early and went to Saul. "Blessed be the Lord," Saul told Samuel. "I have done what he commanded."

"Then why do I hear the bleating of sheep and the lowing of oxen?" Samuel asked. "God commanded you to destroy every living thing in Amalek."

"We saved only the best animals from Amalek," Saul answered. "We wanted to make a sacrifice to the Lord."

"You were a young man, like other young men," Samuel said. "Then the Lord chose you to be king of Israel and to lead the people in battle. When he told you to punish the Amalekites, he told you to destroy them completely, to kill every living thing. Why did you disobey the Lord?"

"But I did not disobey him," Saul said. "I destroyed the city and everyone in it, thousands of people. I took only one prisoner — Agag, the king. As for the animals, the people wanted to make a sacrifice to the Lord. I let them do what they wanted because I was afraid of them."

"Do you think the Lord wants sacrifices more than he wants obedience?" asked Samuel. "It is better to obey the Lord than to make sacrifices to him."

"I was wrong," said Saul. "I beg you, please ask the Lord to forgive me." Without listening, Samuel turned to

leave. As he turned, Saul grabbed at his robe to stop him, but the cloth tore off in his fingers.

"Just as you have torn my robe, so the Lord will someday tear your kingdom away from you and give it to someone else," said Samuel. "You have turned away from the Lord, and now the Lord is turning away from you."

So Saul went to his home, and Samuel went to his, and they never saw each other again. But Samuel wept for Saul, because the Lord no longer wanted him to be king.

# David and his Harp

"Do not weep for Saul any more," God said to Samuel. "Go to Bethlehem, for there I have chosen a new king of Israel, one of the sons of a man named Jesse."

So Samuel went to Bethlehem and gathered all the people, to make a great sacrifice. Jesse came and brought all his sons to meet Samuel. Samuel studied each boy carefully. They were all tall and strong and handsome. Still, the Lord had told Samuel not to judge men by how they looked but by what was in their hearts, and Samuel could tell that none of these boys was the new king.

"Do you have any other sons?" Samuel asked Jesse.

"Yes," Jesse answered. "My youngest son, David, is watching the sheep."

"Send for him," said Samuel.

When David came in from the fields, God said to Samuel, "This is the king I have chosen. Give him my blessing."

David was handsome and strong, and his trust in God shone in his eyes. As David stood among his brothers, Samuel poured holy oil on David's head to show David

that God had chosen him to be king one day. At that moment, David felt the Spirit of God fill his heart, and it stayed with him all his life.

But when God turned away from Saul, an evil spirit filled the king. Even on the brightest days, Saul would fall into a bad temper, sometimes for no reason at all. He would sit and stare, and nothing anyone did pleased him. One day, Saul's servants came to him. "Perhaps, my lord, if we found someone who plays the harp and sings sweetly," they suggested, "it would make you feel better and chase the evil spirit away."

"Send me a man who can do that," answered Saul.

"I hear that a man named Jesse has a son who plays the harp and sings beautifully," said one of the servants. "His name is David, and he is a handsome and brave boy who is careful to do everything the right way."

So David came to Saul, and Saul loved him immediately. "Let your son David stay with me," Saul said to Jesse, "for I want him near me to help me."

Saul gave David the job of carrying his armor, and David lived in Saul's house. Whenever Saul felt a dark mood coming over him, he would ask David to play his harp, and the evil spirit would disappear.

David sang many songs, called psalms, and we still sing them today. This is the psalm for which we remember David most:

*The Lord is my shepherd; I shall not want.*

*He makes me lie down in green pastures; he leads me beside the still waters.*

*He restores my soul; he leads me in the paths of righteousness for his name's sake.*

*Yea, though I walk through the valley of the shadow of death, I will fear no evil, for you are with me; your rod and your staff, they comfort me.*

*You prepare a table before me in the presence of my enemies; you anoint my head with oil; my cup runs over.*

*Surely goodness and mercy shall follow me all the days of my life, and I will dwell in the house of the Lord forever.*

Psalm 23

# David and Goliath

The Israelites and the Philistines began fighting again, as they had in Samson's days. All the armies of Israel gathered on one mountain, and the armies of the Philistines gathered on the opposite mountain. Between them lay the valley of Elah.

One morning, the strongest of the Philistines, a huge man named Goliath, came down into the valley. He stood nearly ten feet tall, and his body was covered with heavy bronze armor from head to toe. His spear looked like a tree trunk, and it was tipped with iron. "Men of Israel," Goliath called, "why do we need armies to fight this war? Let one Israelite come forward to fight me. If he wins and kills me, then we Philistines will be your slaves. If I win and kill him, then you will be our slaves."

When Saul and his soldiers heard this, they were afraid. Every morning and evening for forty days, Goliath called out these words to the Israelites, but no one came forward to fight him.

Now three of David's brothers were in Saul's army, but David had been sent home to help his father. One morning, Jesse told David to leave his sheep and take bread and cheese to his brothers. David reached the camp just as

Goliath was repeating his terrifying words. David watched as all the Israelites turned away in fear.

"Have you seen that man?" the Israelites asked one another. "Did you see how big he was? Imagine what the king will give the man who kills Goliath — gold, silver, even one of his daughters to marry!"

"Will Saul really give all that to the man who kills Goliath?" David asked. But no one would answer David. "What are you doing here?" they all said. "Fighting is no business of yours."

When Saul heard that David was in the camp, he sent for him. "Do not be afraid, my lord," David said to Saul. "I will fight Goliath. He is nothing but a boastful Philistine who prays to false gods."

"How can you fight Goliath?" asked Saul. "You are young and a shepherd, and he has been a great warrior all his life."

"When I watch my father's sheep," answered David, "lions and bears sometimes try to steal them. I go after these beasts and grab them by their heads and kill them. If the Lord has saved me from the fierce lions and bears that attack my father's sheep, I am sure he will protect me from Goliath."

The way David spoke convinced Saul to let him fight Goliath. "Go," he said, "and may the Lord be with you."

Then Saul dressed David in his own armor and gave him his sword. "I cannot use these," said David. "They are uncomfortable." David took off the armor and picked five smooth stones from a brook. With these and his slingshot, David went out to meet Goliath.

When Goliath saw David, the Philistine was disgusted. "Am I some kind of puppy, that the Israelites send out a boy with a stick to play with me?" And Goliath cursed David by all the gods of the Philistines.

"You may have a sword and a shield," David answered, "but I have the Lord of Israel on my side. Today everyone will see that battles are not won with swords and shields, but with faith in the Lord."

Furious, Goliath rushed at David. Quickly, David snatched a stone from his bag, slipped it into his slingshot, and let it fly at Goliath. The stone struck the Philistine right in the forehead, and he fell face down on the ground. David ran to Goliath, took out the fallen warrior's sword, and chopped off his head.

When the Philistines saw their hero lying dead, they scattered in terror, running back to their cities. With a great shout, the Israelites ran after them and chased down the fleeing Philistines. Then they destroyed the enemy camp and celebrated their wonderful victory.

# David Becomes King

After David killed Goliath, the army of Israel, with Saul and David at its head, was greeted with joy everywhere. In every town the women would come out and sing, "Saul has killed his thousands, and David his tens of thousands."

These words angered Saul. "They say I have killed thousands of Philistines and David has killed tens of thousands," thought Saul. "Soon the people will want to make him king."

From that moment on, Saul was jealous of David and kept close watch over him. One afternoon a dark mood came over Saul, and David played the harp for him, as he always did. But as Saul sat, holding his spear, he became angrier and angrier. Twice Saul threw his spear at David, but both times David jumped out of the way.

Seeing that the Lord was with David and protected him, Saul was afraid. Finally, he decided to make David leader of a thousand soldiers. Saul hoped David would be killed in battle, but David was a fine commander and was not killed. He acted wisely and succeeded in everything he did, and all Israel loved and respected him.

Then Saul thought of another plan. He knew that
his daughter Michal loved David, and he promised David
that he could marry her if he killed a hundred Philistines.
Saul secretly hoped that in the battle the Philistines would
kill David. Instead, David slaughtered two hundred
Philistines, and Saul had to let him marry Michal.

Now Saul's son Jonathan was David's closest friend.
The two young men were as close as any brothers. But one
day Saul told Jonathan of his plans to kill David. Jonathan
was horrified. "David has done nothing to hurt you," he
told his father. "Why do you want to hurt him?"

Saul listened to Jonathan and promised not to kill David, but he could no longer control his anger and jealousy. After David won another great victory over the Philistines, Saul again hurled his spear at David, and this time David ran from the palace and fled to Ramah. While he was in hiding from Saul, David went secretly to see Jonathan.

"What have I done?" David asked Jonathan. "Why is your father trying to kill me?"

"I am sure he does not want to kill you," answered Jonathan.

"He knows you are my dearest friend, so he has not told you," David replied. "But it is true."

"If this is true and I can help you," answered Jonathan sadly, "I will do whatever you want."

"I thank you," said David. "Tomorrow, I am to have dinner with your father, as I do at the beginning of every month. This time I will not join him. If your father asks you where I am, tell him I have gone to Bethlehem. If he is not angry, that means he does not want to hurt me. But if he does get angry, then we will both know that he thinks of me as his enemy."

Jonathan agreed, and the two young men swore before God to be friends as long as they lived. Before they parted, David asked, "How will I know whether your father is still angry at me?"

"Stay in these fields for two days," answered Jonathan. "On the third day, hide behind that pile of rocks. I will come and shoot three arrows toward the rocks, as if I were shooting at a target. I will bring a young boy with me to pick up the arrows. If I say to him, 'The arrows fell nearby; please go get them,' that means it is safe for you to come out of hiding. But if I tell him, 'The arrows are far away,' you are in danger and must escape at once."

When Jonathan joined his father at the dinner table the next day, Saul did not seem to mind that David was missing. But on the second day, when David was absent once again, Saul asked Jonathan where his friend was. Jonathan said David was visiting his family in Bethlehem.

"You fool!" Saul shouted. "You have chosen David

over your family! As long as David lives, you will never be king. David must die!"

"But what has David done?" asked Jonathan.

Too angry to answer, Saul threw his spear toward Jonathan. Jonathan left the table in a rage.

The next morning, Jonathan went out to the field where David was hiding. "Bring back the arrows I am shooting," he told the boy with him. Jonathan shot an arrow beyond him. "The arrows are far away," he called.

Jonathan then sent the boy home. As soon as he was gone, David came out from behind the rocks. Jonathan and David hugged each other and wept. "Whatever happens," Jonathan said, "let us be friends forever." Then he returned to the city, and David went into hiding.

So it was that David, whom God had chosen to be king of Israel, left his own country. His brothers and his father's household joined him, as did many other men who were unhappy. Altogether, there were about four hundred men, and David was their leader. They fought many battles, and David's fame grew.

As for Saul, he felt that God had abandoned him. He chased David and his men everywhere. Twice Saul's path crossed David's, and each time David could have killed him, but he chose not to. "The Lord will judge between us and decide who is right," David said to Saul after the second time. Saul wept and parted with David, saying, "You have given me good for evil."

After some time, the Philistines raised a huge new army against the Israelites. When Saul saw how many men they had, he feared for his life and for the lives of his soldiers. Samuel had died by this time, so Saul asked God directly what to do. But the Lord did not answer him.

Saul could neither eat nor sleep, as he frantically searched for help. Finally, he traveled to Endor, to seek a witch who knew how to talk to the dead.

"You must raise the spirit of Samuel," he told the witch of Endor. The woman cast her spell, and the spirit of Samuel rose from the earth.

"Why do you disturb me?" asked Samuel.

His voice shaking, Saul told Samuel that the Philistines were preparing for war and that the Lord would not answer his prayers. "What should I do?" Saul asked.

"Why do you ask me," said Samuel, "when the Lord himself is now your enemy? God has given your kingdom to David because you did not obey him at Amalek. Tomorrow you and your sons will be with me, and your army will be at the mercy of the Philistines."

Weary from fear and hunger, Saul fell full length on the ground. He knew that the next day he and his sons would die and that the armies of Israel would be destroyed with them.

Everything happened as Samuel predicted. The armies of Israel fled before the Philistines, and all three of Saul's sons were killed. Wounded by arrows, Saul fell on his own sword and killed himself rather than die at the hands of the enemy.

When David heard the news of the battle and the death of Saul and Jonathan, he wept and tore his clothes. "How the mighty are fallen!" David mourned. "No one was braver than Jonathan, and Saul never turned away from battle. Weep for them, Israel — for Saul, whom God chose to be king, and for Jonathan, who was like my brother."

Then David became king of Israel in Hebron and ruled the country for forty years. During David's reign, the Israelites defeated their enemies and rebuilt their country, which had been torn apart by war. David also captured the city of Jerusalem and made it a holy city. With music and rejoicing, he brought to it the Ark in which were kept the laws that God had given Moses. In time, Jerusalem became known as the city of David. And David became the greatest king of Israel, for the Lord was with him.

# The Judgment of Solomon

David ruled Israel for forty years. When he died, his kingdom passed to his son Solomon. Solomon was a great king who ruled in peace. To show his thanks, Solomon decided to build a beautiful temple to the Lord. It was made with the finest cedar wood from Lebanon and with huge blocks of stone. Solomon decorated the Temple with gold and rich carvings. In front of it stood two great bronze pillars. It took Solomon seven years to build the Temple.

But when the Israelites spoke of King Solomon, they praised his great wisdom, not his wonderful buildings.

Once two women came before Solomon. "My lord," the first woman said, "this woman and I were living alone in the same house when I gave birth to a baby boy. Three days later she also had a baby boy. That night both of us went to sleep holding our babies. But this woman fell asleep on top of her baby, and the poor child died. At midnight she woke up and saw that her baby was not breathing. She crept into my room, quietly took my baby away from me, and put her dead baby in my bed."

"You are lying!" cried the second woman.

"Let the woman finish her story," Solomon ordered.

"When I woke up," the first woman went on, "I discovered the dead baby in my bed, but I saw that it was not my baby. Now I want my baby back."

"Nonsense!" answered the second woman, and the two women argued back and forth while King Solomon looked on. Finally he said, "Bring me a sword."

The king's servants brought him a sword. "Now,"

ordered the king, "cut the baby in two, and give half to each woman. That way both of them will be satisfied."

"No!" cried the first woman, weeping. "Let her have the child. Anything, as long as you do not harm him."

"It is a good judgment," the second woman said. "If I cannot have the baby, at least she will not have him."

For a moment everyone was silent. Then King Solomon spoke. "Give the first woman the child," he said. "She is the mother. She loves the baby so much that she would rather part with him than see him hurt."

When the people heard this judgment, they marveled at Solomon, for they knew the wisdom of God was in him.

# The Prophet Elijah

After Solomon died, his kingdom was divided, and most of the men who ruled were not wise and great leaders. But there were still a few leaders who listened to the words of the Lord and told the people to do what was right. These people were called prophets. One of these prophets was Elijah, who lived while Ahab was king of Israel.

King Ahab was married to a woman named Jezebel, who worshipped the false god Baal. Ahab also turned to Baal, and even built an altar to him. This made God angrier at Ahab than he had been at any other king. Elijah went to Ahab and told him, "As truly as I serve the Lord, there will be no rain in this land until I say so."

For three whole years there was no rain. For these three years, Elijah hid, while the Lord protected him. Then the Lord came to Elijah. "Go, speak to Ahab again," the Lord said, "and I will send rain."

When Elijah came before the king, Ahab asked, "Are you the troublemaker who brought this dryness to the land?"

"You are the one who brought trouble to the people of Israel because you follow false gods," answered Elijah. "Now gather the people and the false prophets of Baal on Mount Carmel."

On the mountain, Elijah spoke to the prophets of Baal and the people. "How long will it take you to decide between God and Baal?" No one answered him. "We will find out today who the true God is," Elijah said. "Let all four hundred and fifty prophets of Baal choose a bull and prepare it for a sacrifice, but let them not make a fire. I will do the same thing. Then we will pray — all of them to Baal, and I to the Lord. The god who answers with fire for the sacrifice is the true God."

The people agreed, and the prophets of Baal built their altar, and laid their offerings on it. From morning until noon they prayed to their god, but nothing happened.

"What is the matter?" asked Elijah. "Is Baal busy talking with someone else, or is he sleeping? Perhaps you should pray louder."

From noon until evening the prophets called out loud, and they even cut their arms with knives to show their love for Baal. Still nothing happened.

"Now come nearer to me," Elijah said to the people. Then he prepared his sacrifice. When the altar was ready, he called for twelve barrels of water, and soaked the wood with them. "God of Abraham, Isaac, and Israel," Elijah prayed, "hear me, so that the people may know that you are the true God and will follow your words once again."

Suddenly a fire came down from heaven, burning up all the meat and wood, and even the stones of the altar and the water. When the people saw this, they threw themselves face down on the ground. "The Lord is our God," they cried.

Then Elijah told them, "Kill these false prophets, every one of them; do not let a single servant of Baal escape." When this was done, a small cloud no bigger than a man's hand formed over the sea. Soon the skies were black with clouds, and a great rain fell.

171

When Ahab told Jezebel what had happened, the queen was furious. She immediately sent word to Elijah that she would have him killed, just as he had killed the prophets of Baal.

So Elijah fled to Mount Horeb, and hid inside a cave, where, exhausted, he fell asleep. When he awoke, a voice asked, "Why are you here, Elijah? Go outside and meet the Lord."

When Elijah went out, the Lord passed by. First, a great wind whipped around Mount Horeb, but the Lord was not in the wind. After that, an earthquake shook the mountain, but the Lord was not in the earthquake. Then, a fire raged over the mountain, but the Lord was not in the fire either. At last, a still, small voice called to Elijah, and that was the voice of the Lord. When Elijah heard the voice, he covered his face with his cloak.

"Why are you here?" the Lord asked.

"I am here because of my love for God," Elijah answered. "The people of Israel have turned away from you. All of your prophets have been murdered. I am the only one left, and now Jezebel wants to kill me."

"Do not be afraid, Elijah," said the Lord. "Those in Israel who bowed down to Baal will be punished. Those who have not bowed down to Baal will be saved. Now you must go and find Elisha, the son of Shaphat, who will be the prophet after you."

So Elijah left Mount Horeb and found Elisha plowing his father's fields. All that Elijah had to do was touch the young man with his cloak, and Elisha knew that the Lord had called him. "Wait while I kiss my mother and father good-bye," said Elisha. "Then I will follow you."

From that day on, Elisha served Elijah, until at last it was time for the Lord to take Elijah up to heaven. The two men were in Gilgal. They traveled to Bethel and then on to Jericho. As they reached each city, Elijah said, "Stay here, Elisha, for the Lord wants me to travel on." But each time, Elisha refused to let Elijah go on alone.

Finally they came to the Jordan River, with a small group of followers. Elijah took off his cloak, rolled it up, and touched the water with it. The waters parted, and Elijah and Elisha crossed to the other side. As they stood by the riverbank, Elijah asked Elisha, "Is there anything you would like from me before I go?"

"I would like to have twice your spirit and faith."

"What you ask for is not easy," said Elijah. "But if you see me as I am taken away, you will have it."

Just then a chariot of fire, pulled by horses of fire, appeared and drove between them. Elijah was carried up by a whirlwind to heaven, and Elisha saw it. "My father, my father!" he cried. "The chariot of Israel and its horsemen!" Then Elijah was gone.

Elisha pulled at his own clothes and tore them to shreds. Then he picked up the cloak that had fallen from Elijah's shoulders and, dipping it into the waters of the Jordan, asked, "Where is the God of Elijah?" As he spoke, the waters parted, and Elisha crossed back to the other side. There he joined Elijah's followers, who saw that the spirit of Elijah was in Elisha and bowed before him.

# Esther, Queen of Persia

In Shushan, the capital of Persia, there was once a king named Ahasuerus. During the third year of his reign, Ahasuerus gave a great banquet for all the princes of his kingdom. When everyone was celebrating, Ahasuerus called his queen, Vashti, to come to him, so all his guests could see how beautiful she was. But Vashti refused. Ahasuerus was so angry he ordered her to leave the palace, and told his servants to find a new queen for him.

Now a man named Mordecai also lived in Shushan, with his beautiful cousin, Esther. Mordecai was not a Persian, but a Jew, a follower of the Lord of Israel.

Ahasuerus's servants searched the whole empire, from India to Ethiopia, to find a new queen, but in the end they found no woman lovelier than Esther. So they brought her to the palace, with many other young women, and presented them all to King Ahasuerus. When the king saw Esther he loved her at once, and chose her to be his new queen. But Esther did not tell Ahasuerus that she was a Jew, for Mordecai had warned her that many Persians did not like Jews.

After Esther became queen, Mordecai often sat by the palace gate so he could see her. One day, as he sat there, he overheard two palace officers plotting to kill King Ahasuerus. Mordecai quickly told Esther, and she ran to the king, who had the two men arrested immediately. Ahasuerus ordered that the whole story be written down in the history of his kingdom.

Soon after this, Ahasuerus made Haman, a rich and proud man, his prime minister. This meant that Haman was the most powerful man in the kingdom after Ahasuerus, and everyone bowed down before him — everyone but Mordecai, for Mordecai would bow down only before the God of Israel. When Haman learned this, he became very angry, and then when he found out that Mordecai was a Jew, he was so furious that he decided to destroy all the Jews in Persia. Haman went to Ahasuerus with his plan. "My lord," he said, "there are certain people who live in your kingdom who are different from us and who do not follow your laws. Why should we let this happen? Let me destroy these people, and I will give your treasury a fortune in silver."

"Do what you think is best," said Ahasuerus.

Immediately, Haman sent letters to every corner of Persia, telling the exact day on which the Jews should be killed.

As soon as Mordecai heard what Haman had done, he sent a messenger to Esther, telling her to go to the king and ask him to save her people. But Esther was afraid. She sent Mordecai a message telling him that anyone who entered the king's inner court without being invited was put to death, unless the king stretched out his scepter toward the person. When he heard this, Mordecai sent Esther another message. "Even you will not escape Haman's orders," he said. "You are the queen, but you are also a Jew, and you will not be saved."

Esther realized that Mordecai was right. "Give Mordecai this message," she told her servants. "Tell him to

gather all the Jews in Shushan and ask them not to eat or drink for three days. I will not eat or drink either. Then I will go to the king. If I die, I die."

On the third day, Esther put on her most beautiful dress and went to the king's inner court. Ahasuerus was pleased to see her, and pointed his scepter toward her.

"What do you want?" he asked. "It is yours, even if it is half my kingdom."

"If it pleases you, my lord," Esther answered, "I would like you and Haman to come to a fine dinner I have prepared for you." That night the king and Haman went to the dinner. When they had all finished eating, Ahasuerus again asked Esther what he could give her. "If you enjoyed

this evening, my lord," she answered, "come again with
Haman tomorrow evening."

As Haman left the palace, he felt very happy. The
king had made him prime minister just a short time ago,
and now the queen had invited him to dinner a second
time. Then Haman saw Mordecai standing by the palace
gate, and forgot all his happiness. "I cannot be happy while
that man lives," Haman told his wife and friends when he
returned home that night.

"Order a special gallows built on which to hang him," Haman's wife and friends said. "Then ask the king for permission to hang Mordecai tomorrow afternoon. That way you will be able to enjoy your dinner."

That night, King Ahasuerus could not sleep. To pass the time, he looked over the history of his kingdom. There he read again how Mordecai had saved his life by telling Esther of the plot against him. "What honor have we given to Mordecai to reward him?" Ahasuerus asked his servants.

"Nothing," they answered.

Just then Haman came to see the king. "Tell me," Ahasuerus asked Haman, "if the king wanted to reward someone, how should he do it?"

Haman, sure that the king was talking about him, answered, "The man should be given the king's robes, the king's crown, and the king's horses, and he should be paraded with honor through the streets of Shushan."

"Excellent!" said Ahasuerus. "Get my clothes, and see that all this is done for Mordecai the Jew. Do not forget anything."

Haman was very angry, but he had to do what the king wanted. Then he went to the dinner Queen Esther had prepared. After they had eaten, the king asked Esther for the third time what she wanted.

"O, my lord," Esther said, "please spare my life, and the lives of my people."

"What do you mean?" asked Ahasuerus. "Are you not my queen?"

"Yes, I am your queen," answered Esther, "but I am also a Jew, and there is a man in your kingdom who wants to kill all the Jews in Persia."

"Who is this man?" demanded the king.

"This wicked man is Haman," Esther answered.

When he heard this, Haman rushed to the queen to beg her for mercy. But the king thought Haman was trying to hurt Esther.

"Will you hurt my queen in my own palace?" Ahasuerus shouted. "Guards, take this man away."

"My lord," said one of the servants, "Haman has built a special gallows on which to hang Mordecai."

"Then hang Haman there," Ahasuerus ordered.

So Haman was hanged that night, on the same gallows he had built to hang Mordecai. The next day, Ahasuerus made Mordecai the prime minister, and gave him all the power that Haman had once held.

Then Esther told Ahasuerus about the letters that Haman had sent to all the princes in the kingdom. "Write to them all, and seal the letters with my ring," said Ahasuerus. "Tell them that all the Jews are to be spared and that they are to live in freedom in my kingdom."

So in this way Queen Esther saved her people, and brought joy and honor to the Jews of Persia.

# The Story of Job

In the land of Uz there lived a man named Job who had seven sons and three daughters. He owned seven thousand sheep, three thousand camels, and hundreds of asses and oxen. Job was a good man, and he led a rich and happy life.

Now there came a day when all the angels of the Lord presented themselves before him, and Satan was among them. "Where have you been?" God asked Satan.

"I have been roaming over the earth," he answered, for he would go through the world, looking for people who could be turned to evil.

Then the Lord said to Satan, "Have you considered my servant Job? There is no one else in the world like him, no one who loves God and hates evil as much as he does."

"He has every reason to love you," Satan answered. "He is a comfortable and happy man. He has everything a man could want. But take away all his riches and his family, and he will curse you to your face."

"Very well," said the Lord. "You may test Job. You may take away everything he has, only do not harm his body in any way."

Soon after, as Job sat by himself, a messenger ran up to him. "The Sabeans have stolen your oxen and asses, and killed all your servants," the messenger cried. "I alone escaped to tell you."

Before the man could finish speaking, a second messenger ran up to Job. "A fire came down from heaven," he said, "and burned up your shepherds and all their sheep. I alone escaped to tell you."

Before the second man could finish speaking, a third messenger ran up. "Three bands of Chaldeans took away your camels, and killed all the men who were with them. I alone escaped to tell you."

Before the third man could finish speaking, a fourth messenger arrived. "Your sons and daughters were eating in your oldest son's house," he cried, "when a great wind came from the wilderness. It blew down the house and killed all your children. I alone escaped to tell you."

Then Job tore at his clothes, and fell to the ground to pour out his sorrows to the Lord. "I came into this world with nothing, and with nothing I shall leave it. The Lord has given, and the Lord has taken away. Blessed be the name of the Lord." In all this Job did no evil, and did not curse God.

The next time the angels of the Lord presented themselves before him, Satan was again among them.

"Have you considered my servant Job?" God again asked Satan. "You moved me against him, although he was perfect in every way, and still he follows my words."

"Skin for skin," answered Satan. "A man will give up everything to save his own life. Cause him enough pain, and he will curse you to your face."

"Very well," said the Lord. "Do anything you want to him, but do not kill him."

Soon Job was struck with a painful skin disease. Sores covered his body, from his feet to his head. He sat all day long in a pile of ashes, scraping himself with a piece of a broken pot. When Job's wife saw how he was suffering, she said to him, "What good is your faith in the Lord? Curse God, and die!"

"You are talking foolishly," Job said. "Are we to take

186

the good things from God and not the bad?" And Job did not curse God.

Hearing of Job's troubles, three of his friends came to visit him. At first, they did not recognize Job. Then, seeing his suffering, they wept and tore their clothes. For seven days they sat with him and did not say a word. At the end of the seven days, Job cursed the day he was born.

Job's friends then tried to help him. "Will you listen to us?" Eliphaz asked. "You know God does not punish people for no reason. You must have done something wrong. Seek God out, and ask him to forgive you. God may wound, but he also heals. This is what you should do."

"O, that all my sorrows could be counted and weighed against my misery. Surely, my pain outweighs my mistakes," Job cried. "You say you are my friends, but you do not comfort me. You tell me I have done wrong when I have not."

"Do not go on like this," said Bildad. "God does not make mistakes. Seek him out, and ask his forgiveness."

"Do not think you are without blame," said Zophar, Job's third friend. "God has great wisdom and knows all the wrong things men do."

"You laugh at me," answered Job. "But I know as much as you know, and I know I have reason to complain. I also know God does not hear me and that my friends do not comfort me. I only want to know why God has done these terrible things to me. I have followed God's commandments, I have helped my neighbors and friends. Now they turn from me, and God does not hear me. I must know why."

When Job and his friends had finished arguing, the Lord came to Job in a whirlwind. "What will you learn from your friends? Come, stand up like a man, for now I shall question you, and you shall answer," said the Lord.

"Where were you when I created the earth, when the morning stars sang together, and all God's children shouted with joy?

"Have you shut the sea in with doors, and said, 'Thus far shall you come, and no farther, and here shall your proud waves be stopped'?

"Do you know where the light gathers, and where the darkness makes its home?

"Do you teach the lion to hunt its prey, and does the hawk fly by your wisdom?

"Have you an arm like God, and can you thunder with a voice like mine?

"Will you find fault with the Almighty? First answer my questions, if you would have me answer yours."

Then Job bowed his head, and was ashamed. "Lord," he said, "I am nothing. How can I answer you? I have spoken about things I do not understand. I will put my hand on my mouth, and say nothing more."

God was pleased by Job's answers and knew that Job now understood the power and greatness of the Lord. He told Job to forgive his friends for the way they had spoken, for they did not really understand the ways of the Lord. Then the Lord gave Job twice the wealth he had before. Seven more sons were born to him, and three daughters. Job lived to be a very old man and died happy, full of knowledge and perfect in his understanding.

# Daniel in the Lions' Den

In the third year of the reign of the Jewish King Jehoiakim, Nebuchadnezzar, king of Babylon, attacked Jerusalem, the city of the Jews, and conquered it. After he conquered the city, Nebuchadnezzar told his chief servant to choose from among the captured Israelites the handsomest and most able young men. These young men he taught the language of the Babylonians, so they could serve in his court.

Among those chosen to serve Nebuchadnezzar was a young man named Daniel, to whom God had given great knowledge and understanding. After Nebuchadnezzar died, Daniel also served his son Belshazzar.

One night, King Belshazzar gave a splendid feast for a thousand guests. While everyone was eating and drinking, a mysterious hand suddenly appeared. In silence it wrote four strange words across the wall of the palace: *Mene mene tekel upharsin.*

Trembling, the king called in his wise men to explain the mysterious writing, but none of them could understand the words. Then the queen remembered that Daniel could explain dreams and signs. "Send for Daniel at once," ordered Belshazzar.

When Daniel saw the strange words, he knew their meaning at once. "You have worshipped gods of silver, gold, and brass, of iron and wood and stone," Daniel said. "But you have not praised the true God, who holds your life in his hands.

"Here, then, is the meaning of the four words. *Mene, mene,* God has decided to end your rule. *Tekel,* God has seen that you have not led a good life. *Upharsin,* your kingdom will be divided after your death."

That night, Belshazzar was killed, and Darius became king.

King Darius picked one hundred and twenty princes to rule his kingdom, and three presidents to rule the princes. Of these, Daniel was the most important. But the

princes did not like being ruled by Daniel, for he was
both a foreigner and a Jew, so they began to plot against him.

One day, the princes came to Darius. "O king," they
said, "these are hard times for Babylon. There are many
people asking the gods for different things in different ways

and in different languages. No wonder our lives are confused. But we have thought of a way to put an end to this confusion. You should make a new law that says that for the next thirty days no one may ask a favor of any god or any man but you, our great and wise king."

"But what happens if someone prays to other gods?" asked Darius.

"He will be thrown into a lions' den," the princes answered. Darius took the advice of the princes and signed the new law.

Now the princes of Babylon made this law because they knew that Daniel would surely break it. Each day he prayed three times to the God of Israel. But the king did not know this.

When Daniel heard about this new law, he went into his house, kneeled down, and gave thanks to God, as he always did. The princes watched Daniel, then rushed to the king. "You must punish Daniel," they said. "He has broken the new law."

The king was very upset at this, for he loved and trusted Daniel. He spent many hours trying to think of some way to spare Daniel. But the princes kept reminding the king that in Babylon no law could ever be changed, so the king ordered Daniel thrown into the lions' den.

"Your God, whom you serve so well, will find a way to save you," said Darius, as his soldiers closed the mouth of the cave with a stone. Then the king went back to his palace. He could not eat and did not sleep that whole night. As soon as the sun rose, Darius rushed to the lions' den.

"Daniel!" he cried. "Daniel, was your God able to save you?"

"O king, may you live forever!" called a voice from deep inside the cave. "My God sent an angel to shut the lions' mouths, so no harm came to me."

The king was so happy that he could hardly wait for his soldiers to open the cave. To punish the princes who plotted against Daniel, Darius ordered them thrown into the lions' den. Then he sent a letter to everyone in the kingdom, saying, "Let every man in my kingdom respect the God of Daniel, for he is the living God who has saved Daniel from the lions."

# Jonah, the Prophet

One day, God spoke to his prophet Jonah. "Go to Nineveh," he said, "and warn the people there that I will destroy them if they do not turn away from evil."

But Jonah did not want to go. "If I go to Nineveh and tell the people that God will destroy them," he thought, "they will turn away from evil. Then God will forgive them and save their city. Why should I make a long and tiresome journey when God plans to save Nineveh anyway?"

So Jonah decided to escape from the Lord. He went first to Joppa, and there boarded a ship headed for Tarshish. After the ship set sail, God sent a terrible storm. The waters rose so high the sailors thought the ship would break in two. They threw all their things overboard, and each man prayed to his own god to stop the storm.

The storm became wilder, and the sailors noticed that Jonah was not on deck with them. Finally they found him fast asleep in his cabin.

"How can you sleep when the ship is in trouble?" shouted the captain. "Get up on deck, and ask your God to help us."

So Jonah went up, but the storm continued to rage.

"Come," said the sailors, "let us draw lots to see who has brought this evil on us."

The lot fell to Jonah. "Who are you?" the sailors asked. "Where do you come from?"

"I serve the Lord of Israel who made the sea and the dry land," answered Jonah. "I thought I could run away from him, but now I know I cannot. This storm is my fault. If you want to save your ship, you will have to throw me into the ocean."

The sailors did not want to throw Jonah overboard, and they rowed harder and harder. But it did no good. Finally there was nothing else they could do. Asking the Lord to forgive them, they tossed Jonah into the sea. The storm stopped almost immediately, and the boat made its way safely to Tarshish.

Jonah sank into the sea like a stone. But the Lord sent a great fish to wait for him, and it swallowed Jonah as he fell to the bottom of the sea. For three days and three nights, Jonah was trapped in the belly of the fish, alone and afraid. But still Jonah thanked God that he was alive. From the bottom of the sea, his prayers reached the Lord, who

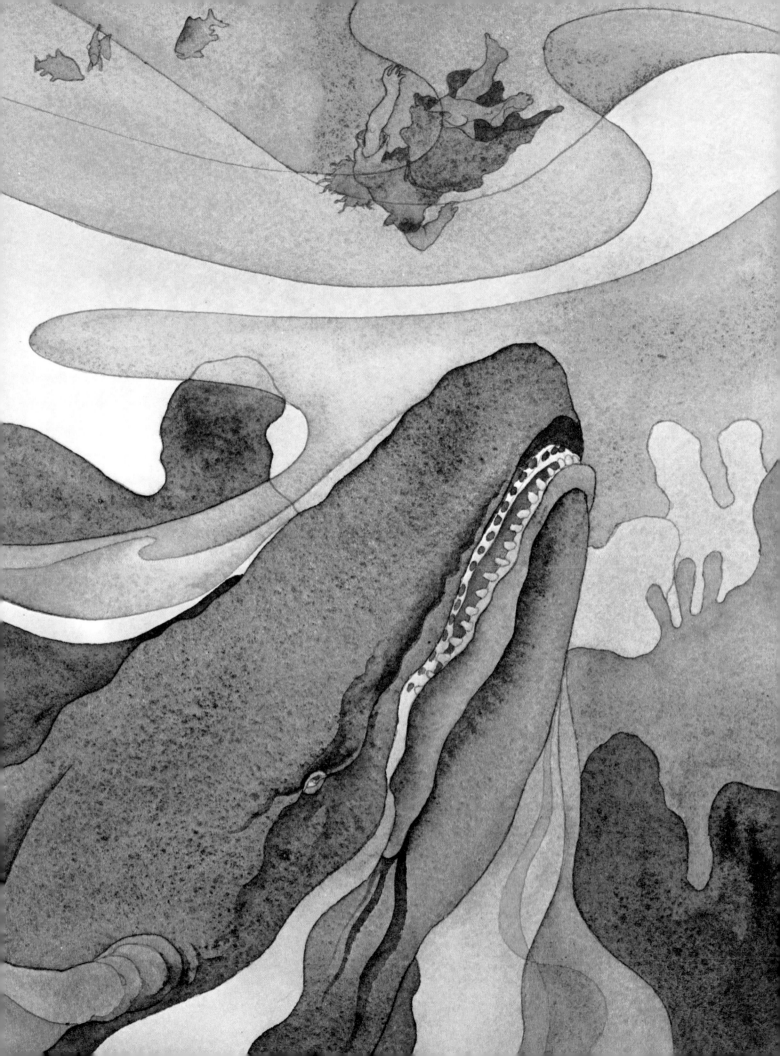

guided the fish toward land. There it coughed Jonah out onto dry land, alive and unhurt.

Then the Lord again told Jonah to go to Nineveh. So Jonah went, as the Lord had asked. With fiery words, he told the people of Nineveh that they had followed evil ways. In forty days, Jonah warned, God would destroy their city. The people of Nineveh saw the truth in Jonah's words, and turned away from evil and violence. When God saw this wonderful change in the city, he decided to spare it.

"Why did you bother to send me here if you knew you were going to save the city?" Jonah complained. "You told me to say that Nineveh would be destroyed in forty days. Now that you have changed your mind, I look like a fool. Please, take my life away. I would rather die than live."

But the Lord asked Jonah, "Do you really have any right to be so angry?"

Still angry at the Lord, Jonah left Nineveh and built a hut, where he waited to see what would become of the city. Then God made a leafy vine grow over the hut to shade the sun, so that its heat would not bother the prophet. But the next morning, the Lord sent a worm to attack the vine, and it withered in the heat of the day. The hot winds blew, and the sun beat down on Jonah, making him feel faint. "Please, Lord," he cried, "let me die."

"Is it right that you should be so angry because of the death of this vine?" asked the Lord.

"Yes," said Jonah. "I should be angry."

Then the Lord said to Jonah, "Look at how much pity you have for this one vine. You did not plant it. You did not make it grow. The vine came up in a few hours and died in a few hours. So should I not have pity for the people of the great city of Nineveh? Think of the thousands of people—think of the children—who would all die if I destroyed Nineveh. Should I not pity them?

"These are my people, Jonah. I have brought them up, and I have seen them turn from evil to good. Should I not pity them, and spare them?"

So Jonah came to understand God's ways and how much he loved his people, and Jonah was glad that Nineveh was saved.

# The New Testament

# The Birth of Jesus

In the land of Judea, in the days when Herod was king, there lived in the town of Nazareth a young woman named Mary. She was promised in marriage to a carpenter named Joseph, who belonged to a family that was descended from David, the great king of Israel.

One day, some time before Mary's marriage to Joseph, the angel Gabriel, sent by God, appeared to Mary as she sat in her house. "Hail, most favored one, the Lord is with you," he told her. "Blessed are you among women."

The angel's greeting confused and troubled Mary. "Do not be afraid," he said to her. "You have found favor with God. Soon, you will have a son, and you shall call him Jesus. He will be great, and his kingdom will have no end."

Mary was more confused than ever. "How can this be?" she asked the angel. "I am not yet Joseph's wife."

"The Holy Spirit will come to you," the angel
answered. "The son born to you will be holy, and he will
be called the Son of God."

Then the angel told Mary more surprising news.
Her cousin, Elizabeth, who was much older than Mary, was
having a child. For years, she and Zacharias, her husband, had
been without children, but now at last they were expecting
a baby. "With God, all is possible," said the angel to Mary.

204

"I am the servant of the Lord," Mary answered. "Let it happen as you say." When she looked again, the angel was gone.

Mary told no one of the angel's visit, but one morning soon after, she went up into the hill country to visit her cousin. Just as the angel had said, Elizabeth was expecting a child. As Mary entered the house, the baby leaped in Elizabeth's womb. Elizabeth was filled with the Holy Spirit, and suddenly she knew about Mary's baby, and who the child was to be.

"You are blessed among women, and blessed is your child," was Elizabeth's joyful greeting to her young cousin in the doorway.

Mary's faith in God grew strong, and she was troubled no longer. "My soul praises the Lord, and I rejoice in God," she returned her cousin's greeting. "For he has done great things to me. From now on, all people will call me blessed."

Mary stayed with Elizabeth and Zacharias for three months, then went home to Nazareth. Soon after, Elizabeth's child was born, a son, whom she and Zacharias called John.

One night in Nazareth while Joseph slept, an angel appeared to him in a dream. "Take Mary as your wife," the angel said. "She is carrying a child, but it is of the Holy Spirit. You shall call him Jesus, for he will save people from their sins."

So Joseph and Mary were soon married, and the time for the birth of the child drew near.

The kingdom of Judea, in those days, was under the rule of the Romans. The Jewish people followed their own customs, but they had to obey the laws made by the Romans. From the Emperor Augustus, a command went out announcing a new tax. Each man was to go to the place of his birth and register there for the tax.

So Joseph left Nazareth with Mary and traveled to Bethlehem, where the family of King David had lived. The little town was crowded with visitors like Joseph and Mary. Any minute now, Mary's child was to be born, but Joseph and Mary could find no room in any of the inns. Finally, a kindly innkeeper offered them a stable to shelter them for the night.

There Mary gave birth to her son. She wrapped the baby in soft swaddling clothes and laid him in a manger to sleep.

Not far away, some shepherds were watching over their sheep in the fields. They looked up and saw an angel of the Lord coming down to them. The glory of the Lord shone all around, and the shepherds were afraid.

"Do not fear, for I bring you news of great joy," the angel said to the shepherds. "Today a Savior has been born to you—the Messiah who will save all the people. You will find him in Bethlehem, a baby wrapped in swaddling clothes, lying in a manger."

Suddenly, all around, there was the singing of heavenly voices, praising God and saying, "Glory to God in the highest, and on earth peace and goodwill toward men."

Then the angel was gone. "Let us go see this baby that the Lord has told us about," the shepherds said to one another. They hurried to Bethlehem and, after some searching, found the stable where Mary and Joseph were staying with the baby.

After they saw him, the shepherds told everyone, far and wide, about the baby and the angel. Then they returned to their flocks, praising God for what they had heard and seen.

# The Flight into Egypt

Herod, the king of Judea, also heard about the baby, and he was not pleased. One day some wise men from the east came to his palace in Jerusalem. "Where is the baby who has just been born and who will be king of the Jews?" they asked Herod. "We have seen his star in the east, and have come to visit and praise him."

Herod pretended to be as excited as the wise men. "Go to Bethlehem, and when you have found the child, bring me word of him," he told them. "I would also like to go and see this wonderful baby."

The wise men set out from Jerusalem. They followed the star from the east, which traveled across the sky to lead them. Then in Bethlehem, it stopped. The wise men went to the place under the star. There they found the baby with Mary, and fell to their knees to worship him and present him with gold, frankincense, and myrrh.

After visiting the baby, the wise men were warned, in a dream, not to go back to Herod, and so they returned to their own country a different way. Joseph also had a dream. The angel of the Lord appeared to him and told him to take Mary and the baby and flee with them into Egypt. "Stay there until I bring you word," the angel said. "Herod will try to find the child and destroy him." By nightfall, Joseph was on his way to Egypt with Mary and the baby.

When the wise men did not come back to

Jerusalem, Herod realized that they had tricked him. His fury was terrible. He called in his soldiers and gave them orders to kill every child, two years old and under, in Bethlehem and the surrounding country. Jesus was safe in Egypt, but hundreds of children were slain.

Some years later, when Herod himself died, the angel appeared once more in a dream to Joseph. "Arise," he said, "and take the child and his mother home. The king who wanted to kill the baby is dead."

But Joseph was afraid to go back to Judea, so he took Mary and the child to nearby Galilee, to the town of Nazareth. There, Jesus grew up.

213

# JESUS' Childhood

While he was growing up, Jesus helped Joseph in his carpenter's shop. With the other children in Nazareth, he played in the fields, and picked fruit in the orchards. He also studied the teachings of his people — the beliefs of the Jews and the laws that God had given them.

Every year, Mary and Joseph went to Jerusalem to pray in the Temple at the feast of the Passover. When Jesus was twelve, they took him with them to the great feast, the festival the Jews celebrated to remember how Moses led them out of Egypt.

When the festival was over, Joseph and Mary started back to Nazareth. They traveled with many friends and relatives, and it was a full day before they realized that Jesus was not with them. Immediately, they hurried back to Jerusalem to search for the boy.

There, after three days of searching, Joseph and Mary found Jesus in the Temple. He was sitting with the priests and teachers, listening to them and asking them questions. The teachers were amazed at Jesus' knowledge and at his questions, but Mary and Joseph were upset. "Son, why did you treat us like this?" Mary asked. "Your father and I looked everywhere for you. We were so worried."

Jesus turned to his mother. "Why did you look for me?" he said. "Did you not know that I would be in my Father's house?"

Joseph and Mary were surprised by this reply and did not really understand it. But in a few minutes Jesus was ready to leave the Temple, and obediently went home to Nazareth with his parents.

Jesus grew to manhood in that little town, among plain people. He was a good and dutiful son, and Mary treasured him, remembering in her heart all the things he said. And as Jesus grew taller and stronger, he also grew in wisdom and found favor with his neighbors and with God.

# JOHN the BAPTIST

John, Jesus' cousin, left his home and went to live in the wilderness. For food, he ate locusts and wild honey, and he wore a coat of camel's hair, tied with a leather belt. There, in the wilderness, John heard the word of God. So John went from that lonely place out into the towns and villages of Judea, traveling the dusty roads with the message from God.

"I am a voice crying out from the wilderness," he said, like the prophets of years before. "Give up your evil ways. Prepare the way for the Lord. Make a straight path for him."

216

From Jerusalem and all of Judea, people came to hear John and ask him how to prepare for the Lord. "If you have two coats," he said, "give one to someone who does not have any. If you have food, give it to the hungry." He told the tax collectors not to cheat the people, and the soldiers not to bully them. Those who heard his words and wanted to turn away from evil, he baptized, washing away their wrongs in the Jordan River so they could lead better lives.

People began to wonder whether John was the Savior the prophets had said would come to lead the people of Israel and bring peace back to the world. For hundreds of years the Jews had been waiting for the Savior, and now they saw before them this wild and strange man who warned them to be ready for the Lord. Some priestly Sadduccees and some Pharisees came to listen to John. The Pharisees were men who studied the laws of the Jews that God gave to Moses very carefully and were proud that they followed them closely. Because of this, some of them thought they were better than other men.

"Who are you?" the people asked, gathering around John. "Are you a prophet? Are you the Savior?"

"I baptize you with water," he answered, "but someone is coming who is mightier than I. He will baptize you with the Holy Spirit and fire. I am not fit to touch the straps of his sandals."

One day, as John was baptizing people, a young man stood quietly in the crowd, watching him. When the man stepped forward to be baptized, John could only stare. Suddenly, everyone was looking at the two men.

"It is you who should baptize me," John said to the other man, who was Jesus.

"Let it be this way," Jesus told him, and waded into the river. As John baptized Jesus, a dove appeared over Jesus' head, and a voice from heaven was heard, saying, "This is my beloved Son. I am well pleased with him."

So John knew that Jesus was the true Savior, the Son of God, who would teach the people and show them God's way.

# The Temptation of Jesus

After his baptism, Jesus went into the wilderness, for he wanted to be alone and to think about the work he would do in his lifetime.

There he fasted, eating no food for forty days and forty nights. At the end of that time, Satan, the devil, appeared to Jesus to test him.

Knowing how hungry Jesus was from fasting, Satan said to him, "If you are really the Son of God, tell those stones to become bread."

"Man does not live by bread alone," Jesus replied. "A man must also live by following the word of God."

Next Satan led Jesus up to the very top of the Temple in Jerusalem. "If you are the Son of God," the devil repeated, "throw yourself off this roof, for it is said that the angels of God will take care of you and catch you in their arms."

"It is also said that man should not test God's power," answered Jesus. "Man should have faith in God without seeing miracles."

Satan then led Jesus high up on a mountain and showed him the kingdoms of the world, spread below with their great buildings and rich palaces. "All this I will give you, if only you will worship me," the devil promised.

"Go away, Satan," Jesus commanded. "It is written that man should worship God alone."

So the devil went away, for Jesus had defeated him, and angels came to take care of Jesus.

# The Apostles

Jesus went home to Galilee, full
of the power of the Spirit. He
settled in the town of Capernaum
and began to preach. He was
now about thirty years old.

Jesus spoke in the synagogue, where the Jews
worshipped, and he walked the roads from town to town,
talking to all who would listen. "I bring you good news," he
told the farmers and shepherds who stopped to hear him.
"The time has come, and the kingdom of God will be here
soon. Turn away from the wrongs you have done, and
believe in me."

While walking by the Sea of Galilee one day, Jesus
met two brothers who were fishermen. Simon Peter and

Andrew were throwing their nets into the water when Jesus
came over to them. "Come with me," he said. "Now you
catch only fish, but if you follow me and believe in me, I
will make you fishers of men." Trusting Jesus, they left
their nets, their homes, and their families and followed him.

Further down the shore, two more fishermen, James
and his brother, John, the sons of Zebedee, were busy
mending their nets. Jesus called to them, and James and
John went with him, too.

223

These four were the first of Jesus' apostles, men who lived and traveled with him. They shared his daily life, and he showed them how to live and how to carry God's message to all the people.

From the towns and countryside of Galilee and the neighboring regions, Jesus chose more apostles, until the number of his messengers came to twelve.

Matthew was a tax collector. He was sitting one afternoon in the marketplace in Nazareth, going over his books. He was tired of collecting money for the Romans from the people in the town. It was a difficult job, for the Jews did not like living under Roman rule and thought that the men who collected taxes were dishonest.

Looking up from his papers, Matthew noticed a man enter the marketplace, his clothes dusty from the roads. A crowd flocked behind him. Jesus went over to Matthew. "Come with me," he said, and Matthew left his papers and followed.

In this manner the other apostles were chosen — Philip, Bartholomew, Thomas, Simon, James the Less, and Thaddeus. The last apostle was named Judas Iscariot.

These twelve men were farmers and fishermen, men who knew what it was to work hard and to be paid very little. All of them gave up what few goods they had to follow Jesus, to live with him and share his simple meals. They called Jesus "Master" and wanted only to learn from him.

Once while Jesus was traveling with the apostles, a young man in fine clothes stopped him. "What must I do to be ready for the kingdom of God?" he asked. He told Jesus that he kept all of God's commandments — he did not lie, steal, or kill, or desire his neighbor's goods. "Is there anything else I should do?" he asked.

"If you want to be truly perfect," Jesus answered him, "go sell all that you own, give it to the poor, and follow me. Then you will have riches in heaven."

The young man was very wealthy, and did not want to give up everything he owned. Sadly, he turned away and went on with his journey. "It is easier for a camel to pass through the eye of a needle, than for a rich man to enter the kingdom of God," Jesus remarked to the apostles.

# The Wedding at Cana

Jesus was invited to a wedding in Cana, another town in Galilee. The apostles were invited, too, as well as Mary, Jesus' mother. The wedding party was very gay, with good food to eat and wine to drink, and music and dancing. But before the party was over, the wine ran out.

"There is no more wine left," Mary said to her son at their table.

Standing nearby were six large water jars. Jesus knew it would spoil the party if there was no more wine, so he called over the servants. "Fill those jars with water," he told them.

The servants filled the jars to the top. "Now pour out a cup for the chief servant to taste," Jesus said.

The servants poured some of the water into a cup and took it to the head servant. He sipped the water, which had been turned to wine, and was delighted with it, although he had no idea where it had come from.

"You are a fine host," the chief servant said to the bridegroom as he served the wine to the guests. "Most people drink the best wine first, then serve the weak wine when they think the guests have drunk so much that they will not know good wine from bad. But you saved the best wine until now."

The guests began dancing and drinking again, and the feast went on. This was the first of Jesus' miracles, and his apostles believed in him more than ever.

227

# Curing the Sick

The good news about the coming of God's kingdom traveled quickly, and crowds began to gather wherever Jesus went. In these crowds there were often sick people who hoped that Jesus would cure them.

One Sabbath, Jesus went to the synagogue in Capernaum to preach. The worshippers were impressed by the strength of what Jesus said and by his faith in God. Suddenly, a man pushed his way up to Jesus. "What do you want here, Jesus of Nazareth?" he shrieked. "Have you come to destroy us?"

At that time, people thought that evil spirits could find a home in someone's body and make him act wildly. So Jesus looked at the man calmly. "Be gone," he ordered the evil spirits. At Jesus' words, the man fell to the floor, shaking and crying. When he got up, he was quiet.

From the synagogue, Jesus and the apostles went for supper to the house of Simon Peter's mother-in-law. She lay in bed, sick with a fever. Jesus took her hand and held it for a moment. The woman rose from her bed, the fever gone, and went to prepare supper.

By sunset that evening, the sick and the suffering of the town had heard of the healings and gathered outside the house. Jesus went out to them. He laid his hands on them, and the sick were cured, the lame could walk again.

The next morning, Jesus began his travels again. On the road he met a leper, a man who suffered from a terrible disease that left his body covered with sores. Because of their disease, lepers were not allowed to go near other people.

The leper knelt down before Jesus. "If only you will, you can make me well," he begged. Jesus stretched out a hand to him. "Be well," he said, and the leper was cured.

Word of these miracles spread everywhere, and when Jesus returned to his house in Capernaum, the street outside was so crowded with people who wanted to be cured that no one could get near it. In the crowd was a paralyzed man, a man who could not move. He was carried on a stretcher by four friends. The door to Jesus' house was blocked by people, and the man's friends did not see any way to get him to Jesus. Finally, they had an idea. They climbed to the roof and removed the tiles above the room Jesus was in. Carefully, they lifted the man to the roof and gently lowered him through the hole they had made.

It touched Jesus to see how much the paralyzed man wanted his help and how much he and his friends believed in Jesus. "Go, your sins — your wrongs against God — are forgiven," he said to the paralyzed man.

Some teachers of the law were standing near Jesus' house at the time, and they were shocked by his words.

"Who is he to forgive sins? Only God can do that," they said to themselves.

Jesus knew what the men were thinking. "You think I am just saying, 'Your sins are forgiven,' but I will show you that I really do have the power to forgive sins on this earth." Turning to the paralyzed man, he said, "Take up your stretcher and walk."

The man got up, took his stretcher, and walked away from the house. Everybody marveled at this and praised God, saying, "Today we have seen something we have never seen before."

# The Sermon on the Mount

These wonderful cures were talked about all over Galilee, and people from Jerusalem and the rest of Judea, from the towns near the seacoast and from faraway Syria, came to listen to Jesus. People with every kind of disease crowded around him, hoping to be cured.

One afternoon, seeing a huge group of people, Jesus climbed to the top of a hill. The apostles sat around as he spoke to the people. He taught them this:

"Blessed are the poor, for the kingdom of God is theirs.

"Blessed are those who are sad, for they shall be comforted.

"Blessed are the gentle, for the whole world shall belong to them.

"Blessed are those who hunger to see justice done, for they shall be satisfied.

"Blessed are the kind and good, for kindness and goodness shall be shown to them.

"Blessed are the pure in heart, for they shall see God.

"Blessed are those who make peace, for they shall be called the children of God.

"Blessed are those who suffer for what is right, for the kingdom of heaven is theirs."

In silence everyone listened to Jesus' words. He spoke for a long time. "I have not come to strike down the laws Moses gave to the people of Israel and the words of the great prophets, but to tell you that you must follow all of them and do still more.

234

"You have been told that if someone hurts you, hurt him in return — an eye for an eye, a tooth for a tooth," Jesus said to the crowd. "But I tell you not to strike back at the man who does wrong to you. If someone hits you on one cheek, turn the other cheek to him. If he takes away your coat, give him your shirt, too.

"You have been taught to love your neighbor and hate your enemy. I tell you to love your enemies as well as your neighbors. Do good to those who hate you; wish good luck to those who wish you bad.

"Pray for those who treat you unfairly. Give something to everyone who asks you. Treat others the way you want them to treat you.

"It is not hard to be good to the people who love you, so do not expect to be rewarded for that.

"Do not count on the treasures you store up on earth, for they will wear out or be stolen by thieves. No, place your faith in good acts that can be stored in heaven. And do not worry about what food you will eat or what clothes you will wear.

235

The birds do not worry about where their food comes from, yet God feeds them. The lilies in the fields do not worry about how they look, but King Solomon in all his glory did not look more splendid. If God feeds the birds and dresses the fields, surely he will take care of every person. Trust him.

"Do not judge other people, saying what they do is wrong, and you will not be judged. Forgive others, and God will forgive you. Give, and much will be given to you. Let there be no limit to your goodness, for God's goodness has no end. And do not make a great fuss over your good acts and call them to everyone's attention. Keep your kindnesses a secret, and God will see them.

"When you pray, pray quietly, by yourself. God knows what you want even before you ask him, so say a few simple words like this:

> *Our Father, who is in heaven, may your*
> *name be honored.*
> *Your kingdom come, your will be done, on earth,*
> *as it is in heaven.*
> *Give us this day our daily bread.*
> *And forgive us our debts, as we forgive*
> *our debtors.*
> *And lead us not into temptation, but deliver us from evil,*
> *for yours is the kingdom, and the power, and*
> *the glory, forever. Amen.*

When Jesus finished speaking, the people were amazed. He spoke like a man with true knowledge, not like a teacher who repeated the words of others.

# Jesus Calms a Storm

One day, Jesus preached to crowds who had gathered at the edge of the Sea of Galilee. There were so many people that Jesus asked the apostles to row him out onto the lake where everyone could see him.

Evening came, and the people, filled with Jesus' words, went home. Jesus and the apostles continued across the lake to the other side. Soon it was pitch dark. Suddenly a terrible storm blew over the waters. Thunder roared and lightning flashed. The waves rose like mountains, and the small boat tossed wildly.

Through the storm Jesus lay sleeping peacefully in the back of the boat. The waves grew higher and higher, and the apostles were afraid the boat would tip over. Waking Jesus, they called, "Master, we are sinking. Do you not care if we drown?"

Jesus stood up. "Be still," he said to the leaping waves and furious winds. At his word, the waves went down, and the sea grew calm. Jesus looked sternly at the apostles. "Why were you afraid?" he asked. "Have you no faith in me?"

The apostles looked at Jesus with wonder. "Who can this man be that the wind and water listen to him?" they asked.

When they arrived on the other side of the lake, in the country of the Gadarenes, a wild man with no clothes on ran up to Jesus and fell at his feet. "Leave me alone, Jesus," he screamed. "Do not make me suffer."

The man could feel that Jesus was already ordering the evil spirits to leave him. These spirits often entered the man and made him so violent that the townspeople chained him up. But he broke the chains and ran off screaming.

"What is your name?" Jesus asked.

"Legion," replied the man, for legion meant many, and he had many evil spirits in him.

Nearby, a herd of pigs stood eating. The evil spirits begged Jesus not to send them into the air, but to let them enter the pigs. Jesus agreed. So the evil spirits left the man and entered the pigs. As they did, the pigs began running around madly, grunting and snorting, until they did not know what to do and jumped into the sea and drowned.

The man who took care of the pigs could hardly believe what he saw and rushed to tell everyone in the town. When the people of the town came down to the seashore, they were amazed to see the wild man sitting quietly with Jesus, fully dressed and in his right mind. But they were afraid of Jesus' power and asked him to leave.

So Jesus returned to Galilee, and the wild man, now cured, went back home and told everyone what God had done for him.

# Jesus Meets the Pharisees

On their travels, Jesus and the apostles ate wherever they could. Often it was at the side of a road or in the fields or the village squares or the house of a friend. If it was getting dark and there was no place to stay nearby, Jesus and the apostles would sometimes go to the first inn they came across for their evening meal.

The Pharisees were shocked that Jesus would sit down and eat with the rough and dishonest people who went to the inns. They themselves ate only with people who kept God's laws about eating, and they washed carefully before touching food, which was prepared in the proper way.

"If you are a man of God," they said to Jesus, "how can you eat with people who cheat and lead bad lives?"

241

"It is the sick who need doctors, not the healthy," Jesus replied. "I did not come to help those who live according to God's laws, but to teach those who do not."

Once Jesus and the apostles were hungry, and as they passed through a field, they picked some ears of corn to eat. But it was the Sabbath, and some Pharisees again questioned Jesus. "Why do you gather food on the Sabbath?" they asked. "It is against God's laws."

"God made the Sabbath for man, so he could rest," Jesus explained. "God did not make the Sabbath so that man would have to follow laws. David knew this, and the priests in the Temple know this, for they do God's work on the Sabbath."

But these Pharisees watched Jesus closely, for they believed all God's laws had to be followed strictly. One Sabbath they saw Jesus come into a synagogue. A man with a shrunken right hand was also there. "If Jesus cures this man," one Pharisee said to another, "he will be disobeying God's law by working on the Sabbath."

"Come forward," Jesus said to the man with the withered hand. Then Jesus turned to the Pharisees. "Is it against the law to do good on the Sabbath? If one of your sheep fell into a ditch on the Sabbath, would you rescue it?"

The Pharisees were silent. Jesus looked at them angrily, for their hearts were hard.

"How much better it is to help a man than a sheep. Come," he said to the man, "stretch out your hand." The man stretched his hand toward Jesus, and it was well again.

The Pharisees left the synagogue without saying a word, but later they met together to plot against Jesus.

# Jesus Speaks in Parables

## THE SOWER AND THE SEED

While sitting in a small boat offshore, Jesus told this story to the people gathered on the beach.

"A farmer went out to plant his crops. As he tossed the seeds into the ground, some of them fell on a path, where they were trampled and eaten by the birds. Some fell onto the rocks, where they started to grow. But there was no soil in which they could take root, so they died. Some of

243

the seeds fell into the thorns and were choked when they started to grow. But others of the seeds fell on good soil and grew into fine, healthy plants. When harvest time came, they yielded a rich crop, and the farmer had much grain.

"Now," said Jesus, "let those who have ears hear."

Later, when the apostles were alone with Jesus, they asked him about this story. "That was hard to understand," they said. "Why do you tell such difficult stories?"

"Those who believe in me and want to follow God's word will understand my stories," answered Jesus. "They are parables, and they teach a lesson to those who want to learn. The parable of the farmer sowing his seed shows what happens when different kinds of people hear God's word.

"The farmer is like a messenger from God, who plants his seeds — sends his word — everywhere. You know that there are some people who hear God's word but do not pay any attention to it. They are like the seeds that fell on the path; they will be lost forever. Some people hear God's word and would like to follow it but do not try hard enough. Like the seeds that fell on the rocks, God's word does not take root in their hearts. The seeds that fell into the thorns are choked, just as God's word is choked in the hearts of people who are so worried by life's troubles or so busy with life's pleasures that they cannot take the time to follow it.

"The seeds that fell into the good soil grow into fine and rich plants that bear much fruit at harvest. These are the people who hear God's word and let it grow in their hearts. They are strong and will have many rewards."

## THE WHEAT AND THE WEEDS

Jesus told another parable to explain who will enter the kingdom of God.

"A man planted some good wheat seeds in his fields, but at night, while everyone was asleep, his enemy came and planted some weeds among the wheat. When the wheat began to grow, so did the weeds.

'Master,' asked the man's servants, 'do you want us to pull out the weeds?'

'No,' answered the farmer, 'I am afraid you will hurt the young wheat if you pull the weeds. Let us wait until harvest time. We will gather the weeds first and burn them. Then we will gather the wheat and store it.'

"How do you explain this parable?" asked the apostles.

"Like the farmer, I plant good seeds in my field, which is the whole world," said Jesus. "Then the devil comes and sows weeds. The good seeds — the people who follow God's word — grow up with the bad. But on the day when the world ends and it is time to decide who will live forever in God's kingdom, the angels will come and harvest. The weeds will be gathered and thrown aside. The good will be gathered up into the kingdom of God."

## THE MUSTARD SEED

Jesus also said, "The kingdom of God is like a mustard seed, which is the smallest of all seeds. But when you plant a mustard seed, it grows into a great branching bush, where birds can make their nests. So it is that God's word takes root and grows in the heart of a good man."

## THE WICKED SERVANT

Peter came to Jesus one day and asked, "Master, how many times should I forgive a man who does wrong to me? As many as seven times?"

"Seven times!" exclaimed Jesus. "I say forgive him seven times seventy times. I will tell you why."

"Once there was a king who decided that all his servants should pay him the money they owed him," began Jesus. "The first servant the king called owed him a great

246

deal of money. Since the servant had no money to pay the king, the king ordered him to be sold as a slave.

'Be patient with me, and I will pay you all the money I owe you,' the servant begged. Moved by the man's words, the king told the servant to forget the debt and let him go.

"No sooner was he free than the man went up to a fellow servant who owed him a little money. 'Pay me what you owe me,' he said, seizing the other man by the throat.

The fellow servant had no money and begged for patience, but the man had him thrown in jail, which was the punishment for people who owed money in those days.

"Now the other servants heard about this and were very upset. They told the king what had happened, and he immediately sent for the first servant. 'I forgot your whole debt when you asked me,' said the king. 'Why did you not show your fellow servant the same pity that I showed you?' And the king became so angry that he sent the man to prison until his whole debt was paid.

"So," said Jesus, "God will forgive us only if we truly forgive those who do us wrong."

## THE GOOD SAMARITAN

To test Jesus, a lawyer said to him, "I know it is written that man must love God and love his neighbor. But how do I know who my neighbor is?"

Jesus told the lawyer this parable.

"A man was traveling from Jerusalem to Jericho when some robbers attacked him. They stole his money, stripped off his clothes, and beat him. Then the robbers went off, leaving the man for dead.

"Soon a priest came along the same road. He saw the man lying helpless and crossed to the other side to avoid him. A priest's assistant also came along. He, too, crossed to the opposite side of the road to avoid the suffering man.

"Then a Samaritan, a man from another country, came along. The Samaritans and the Jews were not friendly, and usually they did not talk to one another. But when this Samaritan saw the beaten man, he ran to help him. He bandaged the man's wounds, lifted him onto his own horse, and took him to an inn.

'Take care of this man,' the Samaritan said to the innkeeper and gave him some money. 'If you spend more money than I have given you, I will repay you on my way back.'

"Now, I ask you this," Jesus said to the lawyer. "Which of the three men was truly the neighbor of the man who was robbed?"

"The one who helped him, even though he was from another country," the lawyer answered.

"Go, and do as he did," Jesus said.

## THE GOOD SHEPHERD

Jesus told this parable to show God's love for each and every person.

"If a man has a hundred sheep and one wanders away, will he not leave the other ninety-nine on the hillside and go search for the lost sheep?" asked Jesus.

"And when he finds the lost sheep, I tell you this: he is happier over that one sheep than over the ninety-nine who never strayed. He lifts it onto his shoulders and carries it home, calling to his friends and neighbors, 'Come, celebrate with me! I have found my lost sheep!'

"In the same way the Lord cares for every person and wants everyone to turn his heart to God."

In another story about sheep, Jesus said, "I am the good shepherd. I know my sheep, and they know me. When my sheep hear my voice, they follow me. They know I have come to protect them and lead them. Others have come before me to steal my sheep and to destroy them, but my sheep did not listen to them. I have come to give them life, that they may live most fully. I would willingly give my life to save the life of my sheep."

## THE PRODIGAL SON

God also rejoices when someone who makes a mistake learns from it.

"There once was a man who had two sons," Jesus began. "One day, the younger son said, 'Father, I would like to have my part of your property now,' for the sons were to get equal shares of their father's property when he died.

"So the father divided his land between his two sons. A few days later, the younger son sold all his land. Putting the money from the sale into his pocket, he left home and headed for a distant country. There he spent all his money, having a good time and doing foolish things. He did not have a penny left when a famine swept the country.

"To keep himself alive, the young man went to work for a farmer taking care of the pigs. He would have been glad to eat the cornhusks the pigs were given, but no one offered him anything.

'My father's servants have more food than they can eat, and here am I, starving to death,' the young man thought to himself. 'I will go home and say, "Father, I am not good enough to be called your son. I have wronged God, and I have wronged you. Treat me like one of your servants."'

"Full of sorrow, the younger son set out for home. While he was still a long way from his house, his father saw him. He ran to meet his son, grabbed him in his arms, and kissed him.

'Father,' the son said in surprise and confusion, 'I have sinned against God and against you. I am no longer good enough to be called your son.'

"But the father called to all his servants, 'Quick! Bring a robe, my best one, and put it on my son. Put a ring on his finger, and shoes on his feet. Then kill the calf we have been fattening, and let us have a feast.'

"When the older son returned from working on the farm that night, he heard music and dancing. 'What is happening?' he asked one of the servants. 'What is all this celebration about?'

'Your brother has come home,' the servant answered. 'Your father has killed the fatted calf to celebrate.'

"But the older son was angry and refused to go into the house. His father came out and pleaded with him, but he refused. 'For all these years, I have worked hard for you and never once disobeyed you, and you have not given me so much as a goat for a feast. Now my brother turns up after wasting all his money, and you kill a calf for him.'

'My son,' said the father, 'you are always with me, and everything I have is yours. But how could we not celebrate this happy day? It is as if your brother died and then came back to life. He was lost, and now he has been found.' "

In this way Jesus made those who had done wrong understand that it was never too late to return to God's ways. If they were truly sorry and had faith in God, God would forgive them and welcome them into his kingdom.

# Death of John the Baptist

After King Herod died, his son Herod Antipas became the ruler of Galilee. This new Herod was a man who did not respect the laws of his people. Under Jewish law, it was a sin to marry a woman who had once been married to your brother, but Herod fell in love with Herodias, his brother's wife, and convinced her to leave her husband and marry him. John the Baptist spoke out strongly against this marriage, and because of this, Herodias hated him.

Herodias asked her husband many times to kill John, but Herod refused. He knew that John had many loyal followers and was afraid of what might happen if he killed their leader. Finally, however, Herod gave in to Herodias and threw John into prison. There Herod came to know John. The two men had many interesting conversations, and Herod saw that John was a good and holy man. Still, John remained in prison, and Herodias waited for her chance to take revenge on him.

When Herod's birthday came, there was a wonderful party. The most important people in Galilee were invited — rich men, noblemen, and powerful commanders. There was food and drink of all kinds. When the guests had finished eating and were relaxing over their wine, Herodias' daughter Salome presented her gift to Herod. For his birthday she performed a marvelous dance. Herod was so pleased he stood up before all his guests and announced, "I will give you anything you want. Ask me for anything, even half my kingdom."

Salome was thrilled. "Mother," she asked Herodias, "what should I ask for?"

"Ask for the head of John the Baptist," answered Herodias.

Salome went straight back to Herod. "I would like you to give me the head of John the Baptist on a tray," she told him.

Herod was shocked and unhappy, but he could not go back on the promise he had made in front of all his guests. Sadly, he sent for his jailer and gave him the order to take John from prison and behead him.

When Salome received her gift, she gave it to her mother. Then John's followers, who had heard the horrible news, came for his body and buried it.

# Feeding the Five Thousand

When Jesus learned that John had been killed, he rowed off to a quiet place so that he could be alone. But people heard that he was there and came from great distances to see him. The sick came to be cured, and the lame and the blind. Jesus' heart was full of pity for these people, and he went among them, healing and teaching the whole day. The sun began to go down, and night was falling.

The apostles took Jesus aside. "It is getting late," they said. "You had better send the people to a nearby town to find something to eat. They are hungry, and there is no place to buy food here."

"There is no need to send them away," Jesus said. "Share your food with them."

"But we have only five loaves and two fishes for the twelve of us," they protested.

"Bring the food to me," Jesus said. He took the five loaves of bread and two fishes and looked up to heaven. Breaking the loaves, he blessed the food and told the apostles to hand it out to the people sitting on the grass.

There were about five thousand men, with women and children, gathered on the shore that day, and each one had plenty to eat. And when the apostles picked up the leftovers, there were twelve large baskets full.

After everyone had eaten, Jesus told the apostles to go ahead without him to the other side of the lake. He stayed behind, saying good-bye to everyone. When all the people had left and it was dark, Jesus went to a hilltop to be alone and to pray.

During the night, the winds on the lake were strong. The apostles rowed as hard as they could, but the winds were against them. From the hilltop, Jesus could see them struggling.

Toward morning, the apostles saw something walking toward them, on the water. "A ghost is coming," they cried out, terrified.

"Take heart," Jesus called over the water. "Do not be afraid. It is I."

"If it is you, Lord," Peter called from the boat, "tell me to walk on the water to you."

"Come," Jesus called, and Peter stepped out of the boat and began to walk toward Jesus. But the wind blew around him, and the waves slapped at his legs. Suddenly, he grew afraid and started to sink.

"Save me, Lord," he cried. Jesus immediately reached out and caught hold of him. "How little faith you have," he said, climbing into the boat with Peter. The seas calmed, and the winds stopped.

"You are truly the Son of God," the apostles exclaimed, filled with wonder.

They landed the boat at Gennesaret. Soon the men and women of the nearby towns heard that Jesus and the apostles were there, and came down, with their sick. They begged just to touch the edge of Jesus' clothes, and those who did, were cured.

# Jesus and Simon

A Pharisee named Simon invited Jesus to have dinner with him. Simon showed Jesus his place at the table, and Jesus sat down to eat.

While Jesus and Simon were eating, a woman from the town came quietly into the room. Everyone knew this woman, for she had lived a bad life, and they called her a sinner. The people of the town would not talk to her. But she knelt behind Jesus, weeping for her bad deeds. Her tears fell on Jesus' feet, and she bent over, kissing his feet and wiping them with her hair. Then she took a jar of very fine and sweet perfume and poured some over his feet.

Simon watched from a distance. "If Jesus were really

a prophet," he thought to himself, "he would know this woman is a sinner and would not let her touch him."

Looking over at Simon, Jesus could tell what he was thinking. "I have something to tell you, Simon," he said.

"Yes, Master," Simon answered. "What is it?"

"Once there was a money-lender who was owed money by two men. One man owed him five hundred coins, and the other fifty. But neither of them had any money to pay what they owed, so the money-lender told them to forget their debts and go away. Now, Simon, I ask you, which man will love the money-lender most?"

"The one who owed him the most money," Simon answered.

"You are right," Jesus told him. Then turning to the woman at his feet, Jesus continued. "When I came into your home, you did not give me water to wash my feet. This woman washed my feet with her tears. Usually, a host greets his guests with a kiss, but you did not kiss me. This woman has kissed my feet ever since I have been in this room. You did not pour oil over my head, as a host does. This woman has poured sweet perfume over my feet.

"For these reasons, I tell you, Simon, her wrongs, which are many, are forgiven, for she shows much love. Like the man who owed five hundred coins, she has much to be sorry for, and she will be forgiven very much."

"Go in peace," Jesus said to the woman. "Your wrongs are forgiven. Your faith and love have saved you."

But the other guests at the table looked at one another unhappily and said quietly to one another, "Who is this man that he thinks he can forgive sins?"

# Jairus' Daughter

Jesus was at the lakeside one day when a man rushed up to him and threw himself at Jesus' feet. "My name is Jairus," the man said. "My daughter, my only child, is dying. Please, Master, I beg you to come touch her and make her well."

Even as Jairus spoke, a messenger ran up to him. "There is no need to bother the Master," he said. "Your daughter is dead."

"Do not be afraid," Jesus said softly to Jairus. "Have faith." So Jairus followed Jesus, for he was a good man, the head of the synagogue in that town. At Jairus' house, his family and friends had already gathered to weep for the dead child. "What is all this weeping?" asked Jesus. "The child is not dead; she is sleeping."

The mourners laughed at Jesus, and he sent them away. "Now come with me," he said to Jairus and his wife, as he led them into the room where the little girl was lying. She was twelve years old. Jesus took the girl by the hand. "Stand up, my child," he said gently.

The girl rose from her bed and walked. Her astonished parents thanked Jesus and wanted to run out and tell everyone about this miracle. But Jesus told them to keep it a secret and to give their daughter something to eat.

264

Jesus especially loved children. When he traveled, women often lined the road and held up their children for a blessing. One hot afternoon, several women kept calling after Jesus to touch their children. The apostles, annoyed that the women were bothering Jesus, shouted at them to go away.

But Jesus stopped them. "Let the little children come to me," he said, as he gathered the boys and girls around him. One by one, he lifted up the children and talked with them. "The kingdom of heaven is made up of children like these," he told the apostles. "If you do not seek God as simply as a child does, you will never enter heaven."

# The Transfiguration

While Jesus was walking along a road with the apostles one day, he asked them, "Who am I?"

"Some say you are John the Baptist, returned from the dead," answered one apostle.

"Some people think that you are the prophet Elijah, who will come back to earth before the day when the Lord decides who will enter his kingdom and who will not."

"But who do you think I am?" Jesus asked them.

"You are the Savior, the Son of the living God," Peter said.

"You are blessed, Peter," Jesus said. "You did not learn that from any man. My heavenly Father showed that to you."

The other apostles looked on, as Jesus grasped Peter by the arms. This humble fisherman was the first person Jesus had asked to follow him. "Your name was Simon, but I call you Peter, which means rock," Jesus said. "You are the rock on which I will build my church. You will spread my message through the world and carry it to all men. To you I will give the keys of the kingdom of heaven."

These words puzzled the apostles, but they listened carefully as Jesus continued to speak to them. "You must

266

not tell anyone that I am the Savior," he warned. "But because you are all my messengers to the world, I will tell you what is going to happen.

"Soon I must go to Jerusalem, and there I will suffer terrible things at the hands of the chief priests and powerful leaders. I will die like a thief, but after three days I will rise from the dead and live again."

Peter grabbed Jesus' arm. "No, Lord," he cried. "This cannot happen to you."

"You are thinking like a selfish man, Peter," Jesus said. "If you or any man wishes to follow me, he must forget himself and be ready to die, as I will die. For what good is life here on earth, if you cannot live forever in God's kingdom?

"This is my message, and you are my messengers. You have the power to cure people and to forgive sins. I am sending you out into the world, with no food and no money. You will suffer, as I will suffer. But if a man gives his life for my sake, he will win life forever in God's kingdom.

"For I will come back with angels, in the glory of my Father, and I will give each man the reward he deserves.

And I tell you this: There are some of you standing here who will see me enter the kingdom of God."

A few days later, Jesus called Peter, James, and John aside. With them he climbed high up on a mountain, where they could be alone. As Jesus stood before them on the mountaintop, he suddenly changed. His face shone like the sun, and his clothes became as white as light.

Two men began talking with Jesus. One of them was Moses and the other Elijah. As they spoke together, a bright cloud filled the sky above them, and from it a voice spoke, "This is my beloved Son, who pleases me. Listen to him."

At the sound of this voice, the three apostles threw themselves down in terror. When they looked up again, they saw only Jesus. He came over and touched them. "Do not be afraid. Stand up," he said.

On their way down the mountain, Jesus told them not to speak of what they had seen until he had risen from the dead.

The next day, when they came down from the mountain, a crowd was waiting. A man kneeled before Jesus and said, "Lord, please help my son. Evil spirits attack him, and he falls into the fire and the water. I brought him to your apostles, but they could not cure him."

"How little faith you have," Jesus cried. "Bring the boy to me."

The father brought his son, who began groaning and twisting on the ground because of the evil spirit in him.

"If you have faith, everything is possible," said Jesus.

"I have faith," said the father, "but I need your help."

"Go away, evil spirit," ordered Jesus.

The boy stopped moving and lay still. "He is dead," the crowd murmured.

But Jesus took the boy's hand and helped him stand up. "You are well," he said. "Go home with your father."

Later the apostles asked Jesus why they could not cure the boy. "You did not have enough faith," he replied. "You must pray hard to chase out such an evil spirit."

# LAZARUS RAISED FROM THE DEAD

In Bethany, a village near Jerusalem, Jesus had three good friends. Mary Magdalene and Martha were sisters who lived with their brother, Lazarus.

One afternoon Jesus was sitting with the apostles when a message arrived from Mary and Martha saying that Lazarus was very sick. "Lazarus will not die," Jesus said, turning to the apostles. "He will live to show the glory of God."

271

The apostles expected Jesus to hurry to his friend's bed, but Jesus lingered in the countryside for two days, preaching to the crowds. Then he said to the apostles, "Come, let us go to Bethany. Our friend Lazarus is sleeping, and I must go wake him."

"But, Master, if he is sleeping, he will get well," the apostles answered, for they did not want Jesus to go too near Jerusalem. They were afraid that his enemies might harm him.

"Lazarus is dead," said Jesus. "Let us go to him."

In Bethany, Mary and Martha were waiting in their house, weeping. Lazarus had died four days before and was already buried in the family grave. Neighbors were with the sisters, trying to comfort them. As Jesus and the apostles neared Bethany, someone saw them on the road and hurried to the house to say that they were coming. When Martha heard this, she rushed out to meet Jesus.

"Oh, Master," she wept, "if you had only been here, my brother would not have died."

"Your brother will come back to life," Jesus answered calmly.

"I know he will come back to life on the last day, when God decides who will die and who will live forever," Martha said.

"If a person believes in me, he will live forever," Jesus said. "No one who has faith in me will ever die." He turned to Martha. "Do you believe this?" he asked.

"I do, Master," she replied quietly. "I believe you are the Savior, the Son of God who has come into the world."

A great feeling of peace came over Martha, and she went home to her sister. "Jesus is waiting for you," she told Mary. Mary quickly got up and went out to greet him. Her neighbors and friends followed her. She knelt before Jesus. "Master," she cried, "my brother would not have died if you had been here."

Sorrow swept over Jesus, and he wept with Mary. "Please take me to the grave where Lazarus is lying," he asked. Mary, Martha, and all the neighbors went with Jesus to the cave where Lazarus was buried. A large stone had been placed in front of the entrance. "Take the stone away," Jesus said.

"But, Master," Mary reminded Jesus, "my brother has been dead four days."

"Did I not say that if you believe in me, you will see the glory of God?" Jesus asked.

The stone was rolled back. The two sisters, along with their neighbors and friends, watched as Jesus stood at the entrance of the cave. Jesus looked up to God. "Father, I thank you for listening to me," he said. "I know you always hear me, but I want all these people to see and believe that you sent me." Then Jesus raised his voice in a loud cry. "Lazarus, come forth," he called, his words echoing in the silence of the cave.

There was a sound from inside the cave, and then a figure appeared at the opening, still wrapped in burial clothes. It was Lazarus, risen from the dead.

The people who had watched were full of wonder, and many believed in Jesus from that day. The story of the dead Lazarus rising from his tomb was passed from person to person, until everyone in Jerusalem had heard about it.

The chief priests and scholars soon learned about this miracle and did not know what to do. Judea was then part of the Roman Empire, and Pontius Pilate was the Roman ruler there. Pontius Pilate did not bother the Jews very much. He made sure that the tax money was collected, and after that he left them to look after their own affairs and to run the Temple. The powerful chief priests and leaders were afraid that the excitement stirred up by Jesus might change all that. Jesus was a strong leader, and many Jews were following him. "Will the Romans think that Jesus is leading the people against them?" they wondered.

Worried that the Romans might take over the Temple or forbid the Jews to practice their religion, the chief priests and scholars called a meeting. "What can we do?" they asked one another. "If we leave this man alone to preach what he will, the Romans will take away our Temple and destroy our people."

Then Caiaphas, who was the high priest that year, stood up to speak. "It is better for one man to die than for an entire people to be destroyed," he said. From that moment, these men began to plan how they might bring about Jesus' death.

# The Entry into Jerusalem

Jesus did not go to Jerusalem often, for his enemies, the powerful leaders of Judea, were there. But when the feast of Passover was approaching, he called the apostles together. "We are going to Jerusalem," he said. "There all the things that the prophets have written and that I have told you about will happen. I will be handed over to the Roman rulers and condemned to death. I will be laughed at and beaten, and I will die like a thief. Then, after three days, I will come back to life again."

The apostles did not really understand what Jesus meant, but they continued on the road to Jerusalem with him and tried to forget what he said. As the group came into the town of Jericho, they passed a blind beggar named Bartimaeus sitting at the side of the road.

"What is happening?" asked Bartimaeus. "What is all this noise?"

"Jesus of Nazareth is going by," said someone in the crowd.

"Son of David, Jesus, have pity on me," cried the beggar.

"Be quiet. Hold your tongue," said the people in the crowd, but the beggar kept calling.

"Jesus, have pity on me," he shouted even louder.

Jesus stopped. "What do you want me to do?" he asked when the blind man came to him.

"Master, give me back my sight."

"Go, your faith has cured you," Jesus said. At once the man could see again, and he joined the crowd following Jesus down the road.

The group came into Jericho, where a huge crowd was waiting for Jesus. Among them was a man named Zacchaeus, who was very rich. He was eager to see Jesus, but he was too short to look over the heads of all the other people. So Zacchaeus ran ahead of the others and climbed up a sycamore tree. When Jesus came to the tree, he stopped.

"Zacchaeus, be quick and come down," he called. "I must stay with you today."

Zacchaeus climbed down from the tree as quickly as he could. He welcomed Jesus, but the people in the crowd were upset.

"Is Jesus going to be the guest of this sinner?" someone asked, for Zacchaeus was a tax collector who had cheated the townspeople. But Zacchaeus stood firm. "Here and now, Lord, I will give half of everything I own to the poor," he promised. "If I have cheated anyone, I am ready to repay him five times over."

"Today you have been saved, Zacchaeus," Jesus told him. "You will live forever in the kingdom of God, for I have been sent by God to save those who have led bad lives." And Jesus went with Zacchaeus to his house.

The next day Jesus and the apostles drew near the city of Jerusalem. When they reached Bethphage, at the Mount of Olives, Jesus sent two of the apostles ahead.

"Go to the next village," he told them. "As you enter, you will find tied up there a donkey which no one has ever ridden. Untie it, and bring it here. If anyone asks what you are doing, say your Master needs it."

The donkey was found, as Jesus had said, and was brought to him. The apostles spread their cloaks over the animal, and Jesus got onto its back.

Beyond the Mount of Olives, spread over the hills, lay Jerusalem, the holy city, gleaming in the sun. A road led out from the city walls, and lining it as far as anyone could see, were people who had come to greet Jesus. Many waved palm branches, which was the way they welcomed great heroes.

As Jesus went by, the crowds carpeted the road with their cloaks, as if a king were passing.

"All praise to the son of David," the people sang. "Blessings on him who comes in the name of the Lord! Sing praise in the highest!"

The apostles walked behind Jesus, singing with the excited crowds. This was the greeting they had always expected for their Master. The apostles sang joyously, certain that Jesus was beginning his reign over the people of Israel. But some Pharisees were upset by all the noise. "Master," they cried, "tell your followers to be quiet. They are making a disturbance."

"If I told them to be quiet," answered Jesus, "then the stones would cry out welcome."

So Jesus rode the donkey past the city walls and into Jerusalem. Excitement swept the streets. People hurried from every direction, shouting and waving. "Sing praise to the son of David! Hail to Jesus!"

Followed by a mighty stream of people, Jesus rode to the Temple. There he got off the donkey and climbed up the Temple steps. The joyous crowd suddenly fell silent. Jesus entered the Temple courtyard. All around him people were busy. The money-lenders were changing foreign coins for visitors, and peddlers were selling birds and animals for sacrifices.

Jesus came near, and in a sudden rush of anger, he threw over the tables of the money-lenders and the chairs of the bird sellers. "This is supposed to be a house of prayer," he cried, "but you have turned it into a place for thieves." With these words, he drove the money-lenders and peddlers out of the Temple.

The chief priests and leaders stood by but did nothing to stop Jesus, for the people in the Temple were crowding around him, shouting his praise and asking for his blessing. There were blind men and cripples, and Jesus cured them. "All praise to the son of David!" shouted the crowd.

"Do you hear what those people are calling you?" one of the priests angrily asked Jesus.

"I do," Jesus answered, and then he left the Temple to spend the night in Bethany.

Jesus awoke early the next morning and again went to Jerusalem. Once more he was greeted by crowds who followed him into the Temple. When the priests and leaders heard Jesus' words and saw how the people listened to him, they were afraid.

Jesus was teaching that the poor who lived according to God's way would enter the kingdom of heaven before the rich people who were so powerful on earth. He said that those who worked hard and suffered would be welcomed and would rest forever in heaven.

The rich and powerful leaders thought that Jesus was speaking against them. They thought that Jesus might lead the people against them and that the Roman rulers would find new leaders for Judea. So these powerful men decided to make Jesus say something that would anger the

Romans. Then the Romans would arrest him. As part of
this plan, a few Pharisees and powerful leaders came to
Jesus with a question to trap him. "Master, you are an
honest man," they said. "You follow the word of God, no
matter what anyone says. For this reason we would like you
to answer this question for us: Should we pay taxes to the
Roman emperor?"

"Why are you trying to trick me?" asked Jesus, for he knew they wanted him to say something against the Romans. "Bring me a coin, and I will show you the answer."

When Jesus took the coin, he held it up and asked, "Whose head is on the coin?"

"Caesar's, the emperor's," they answered.

"Then give to Caesar what is his, and give to God what belongs to him," replied Jesus.

The leaders were amazed at the wisdom of Jesus' answer and went away. They had failed to trap him.

Among the people in the temple there was a lawyer who had been listening carefully to Jesus. He was very pleased with Jesus' answers and wanted an answer to one of his own questions.

"Master," he said, "tell us which is the most important commandment?"

"The greatest commandment of all," answered Jesus, "is 'You shall love the Lord your God with all your heart, with all your soul, and with all your mind.' And the second most important commandment is this: 'You shall love your neighbor as yourself.' Nothing is more important than these two commandments."

"Master, you have spoken the truth," said the lawyer. "There is nothing greater than to love God and to love your neighbors."

"You are close to the kingdom of heaven," Jesus said, and after that no one asked any more questions.

# The Last Supper

It was only two days until the Passover festival. The chief priests and leaders were more afraid of Jesus than ever, and they met to figure out how they might have him arrested and put to death. "We cannot harm him during the festival," they said, "for the people will riot."

Then Judas, who was one of the apostles, went to the priests. "What will you give me if I help you capture Jesus?" he asked.

They counted out thirty silver coins and gave them to Judas, and he began planning when to hand Jesus over to them.

On the first day of Passover, it was the custom for Jews to celebrate with a special supper.

"Go into Jerusalem," Jesus told Peter and John.

"There you will meet a man carrying a pitcher of water. Tell him, 'The Master says we are to keep Passover at your house.' Then he will show you a large room. You can prepare it for us."

Peter and John found everything as Jesus had said they would, and they prepared the Passover meal. At sundown, Jesus came to the house with the other apostles. He knew this was his last supper with them on earth, and he wanted to tell the apostles many things. Before the meal began, Jesus tied a towel around his waist and filled a basin with water. Kneeling before each of the apostles, he washed their feet.

When it was Peter's turn, the apostle refused. "I will not let you wash my feet, Lord," he protested.

"If I do not wash you, you are not a follower of mine," replied Jesus.

"Then wash my feet, and my hands and my face as well, Lord," Peter said.

When Jesus had washed the apostles' feet, he sat down at the table. "Do you understand what I did?" he asked. "You call me Master, which is right, for that is what I am. But I have acted as a servant to you, and you must act this way with one another. I have set an example for you to follow."

The twelve apostles sat down at the table with Jesus. Suddenly, he looked up at them, his face filled with pain. "I tell you," he said, "one of you is going to hand me over to my enemies."

"Do you mean me, Lord?" they asked, one after
the other.

"It is someone who is dipping his bread into the
bowl with me tonight. It is written that this will happen, but
it would be better for the man who does it if he had never
lived."

"Master, can you mean me?" Judas asked.

"The words are yours," Jesus replied.

Then they ate their supper. Taking some bread, Jesus blessed it and gave it to the apostles. "This is my body," he said. "Eat of it." Next he took a cup of wine and gave thanks to God for it. He passed it to all the apostles, with these words, "Drink from this cup. This is the cup of my blood, which will be shed to forgive the sins of all men." As the supper ended, Jesus gave the apostles his final message. "Tonight, I am going where you cannot follow. I want to leave you with a new commandment: Love one another. If you do this, everyone will know you are my followers."

Supper was finished, and they all sang a Passover hymn before going out into the night. Together they went to the Mount of Olives.

"Tonight, all of you will lose your faith because of what will happen to me," Jesus told the apostles. "But after I come back from the dead, I will meet you all again."

"Everyone else may lose his faith in you, but I never will," Peter promised.

Jesus put his hand on Peter's shoulder. "This very night, before the cock crows to announce the morning, three times you will say you do not know me," he said.

"No," protested Peter, "even if I have to die with you." And all the apostles agreed with him.

Near the Mount of Olives, outside the walls of Jerusalem, was a garden called Gethsemane. Jesus and the apostles went there. "Sit here while I pray," he told them. He took only Peter, James, and John with him. Jesus seemed overcome with sadness.

"My heart is ready to break," he said. "Rest here, and stay awake with me."

Jesus walked a few steps further, then fell face down on the ground in prayer. "Father, if it is possible, do not make me suffer this great and horrible punishment. But I know it must be done as you want, not as I want." Great drops of sweat, like blood, rolled down Jesus' face, so hard did he pray. Near him, Peter, James, and John slept. "Are you asleep?" Jesus asked. "Could you not stay up this one hour with me?"

Again, Jesus went off to pray and, coming back, found the three weary apostles asleep. After he prayed a third time, he came over to Peter, James, and John and woke them. "Up, up, the hour has come," he said. "I am about to be handed over to my enemies."

The three apostles struggled to their feet while the other apostles joined them. Storming up the road came a crowd carrying torches and armed with clubs. With them was a group of Roman soldiers. At their head was Judas Iscariot, one of the twelve apostles.

"The one I kiss is the man you want," Judas explained to the crowd. "Seize him and take him away." He then went up to where Jesus stood with the apostles. "Master," Judas said, kissing Jesus.

"Judas, my friend, do what you must," Jesus said sadly. "But why turn me over to my enemies with a kiss?"

The crowd rushed in on Jesus and grabbed him. Then Peter ran forward and pulled out his sword, striking off the ear of the chief priest's servant. "Put away your sword," Jesus ordered, and he healed the servant's ear.

He turned to the frantic Peter. "If I needed help, I could ask my Father to help me. Would he not send bands of angels to save me?" he asked. "Must I not do what is written?" Jesus drew himself up straight and spoke to the crowd. "I am Jesus of Nazareth," he said proudly. "I am the man you want. But why do you come for me in the dark of night, as if I were a dangerous thief? Everyday I have preached openly in the Temple. Why did you not arrest me there?"

But the soldiers and the police led Jesus away as the frightened apostles fled into the night.

# The Trial of Jesus

The soldiers brought Jesus to the house of Caiaphas, the high priest, where a group of powerful leaders was waiting for him. Peter followed the crowd to the high priest's courtyard, and there he waited in the shadows to see what would happen. He could not stay away from his Master, but he was afraid he would be arrested, too.

The night was chilly, and someone lit a fire in the middle of the courtyard. Peter went over to warm himself. One of the servingmaids from the house noticed him at the fire. "You were with Jesus of Nazareth," she said. "I saw you with him."

"I do not know what you are talking about." Peter answered and moved away quickly. But another woman saw him and said, "This man was with Jesus of Nazareth."

"I do not know that man," Peter insisted and again moved away.

By this time some bystanders had noticed him. "Surely you are one of the men who were with Jesus," they said. "You talk like someone from Galilee."

Peter faced the group angrily. "I do not know the man," he snarled. As soon as Peter said these words, a cock crowed. A chill ran through him, and he remembered Jesus' words: "Tonight, before the cock crows, you will deny me three times." Peter went outside and wept.

During this time the high priest was questioning Jesus. Many came forward to accuse him of crimes he had not committed, but no two people agreed on any crime. Throughout the questioning, Jesus kept silent. Finally the high priest asked, "Are you the Messiah, the Son of God?"

"You have said it," answered Jesus. "But I tell you this: From this time on, you will see me sitting at the right hand of God, in the clouds of heaven."

These words infuriated the high priest. "Do we need to hear more? This man says he is the Son of God. He shows no respect for God. This is blasphemy," shouted Caiaphas, and he ordered his men to tie Jesus up and lead him to Pontius Pilate, the Roman governor.

When Judas saw Jesus being led away, he was filled with sorrow and realized what a terrible thing he had done. Quickly he went to the priests in the Temple and tried to give them back the thirty pieces of silver. "I have sinned," he said. "I have handed over a man who has done no wrong."

"What does that matter to us?" said the priests.

Seeing that he could not undo his awful act, Judas threw the coins on the floor of the Temple and rushed out. That morning he hanged himself.

At the palace Pilate questioned Jesus. To all the charges made against him, Jesus gave no answer. Then Pilate asked, "Are you the king of the Jews?"

"My kingdom is not in this world," Jesus replied. "If it were, would my followers not fight for me?"

"Then you are a king?" asked Pilate.

"You have said it," Jesus answered. "I will only tell you this: I was born to bring the truth to this world."

"What is the truth?" asked the puzzled Pilate as he left the room.

Now at that time it was the custom of the Roman governor, during the Passover festival, to free from prison one man chosen by the people. Among the prisoners in the Roman jail was a man named Barabbas, a murderer and leader of riots. Pilate knew that the chief priests had brought Jesus to him because they were jealous of Jesus, and the governor thought the people might free him.

Pilate went out to the balcony of his palace and stood before the crowd, sure that the people would choose

Jesus over a murderer. "Which man shall I let go, Barabbas or Jesus?" he asked.

"Barabbas," shouted the crowd, for their leaders had sent word ahead, saying which man to choose.

"What shall I do with this man you call king of the Jews?"

"Crucify him!" answered the crowd.

"Why?" called back Pilate. "What has he done wrong?"

But the people in the courtyard were growing restless and only shouted louder, "Crucify him! Crucify him!"

Afraid of what the unruly crowd might do, Pilate decided to please the people. But first he called for a bowl of water. Standing on the balcony, he washed his hands and declared, "See, my hands are clean of this man's blood."

Pontius Pilate went into the palace and ordered the release of Barabbas. He then had Jesus whipped and handed him over to his soldiers to be crucified, for this was the way the Romans punished dangerous criminals.

# The Crucifixion

The soldiers of Pontius Pilate took hold of Jesus and led him into a great hall.

There they stripped him of his clothes and draped him in a robe of purple, like a king. On his head they placed a crown of thorns. Then the soldiers knelt before Jesus and made fun of him.

"Hail, king of the Jews," they laughed, spitting at Jesus and beating his head with a cane. When they had finished mocking Jesus, they ripped the purple robe off his back and put his own clothes on him again.

The soldiers then led Jesus away to be crucified. A

few days before, Jesus had passed through the streets of Jerusalem on a donkey and was greeted with palm branches and treated like a king. Now he walked through the city to his death. He had not slept the night before, and he was weak from hunger.

Beaten and mocked, Jesus stumbled under the heavy wooden cross that he had to carry and fell on the rough cobblestones. In the crowd was a man called Simon, from Cyrene, who was passing on his way from the country. The soldiers took hold of him and ordered him to carry the wooden cross on which Jesus would be crucified. Simon walked behind Jesus on his painful journey. Many people followed, and the women wept over Jesus' cruel punishment.

"Do not weep for me, daughters of Jerusalem," Jesus said. "Weep for yourselves and your children, for evil days are coming."

Now they reached the hill called Golgotha, or Place of the Skull. It was a lonely spot, outside the city walls. Here the Romans brought the guilty to be crucified so all could see and be warned. With Jesus that day were two thieves.

The soldiers offered Jesus a drugged drink to dull
his pain, but after he took one sip, he refused to drink it. So
the soldiers stretched Jesus out on the cross and nailed him
to it by his hands and feet. Jesus lifted up his eyes and
looked at the soldiers. "Father, forgive them, for they know
not what they do," he said in a low voice. But the soldiers
were busy rolling dice to see which one would take home
Jesus' clothes and paid no attention. On either side of him,
they crucified the two thieves.

The soldiers raised the cross and stood it in the hole

that was dug for it. Then they sat down to begin the death watch. Sometimes it took several hours, even days, for a person to die on the cross.

Jesus hung on the cross. Above his head was tacked a sign stating his crime: "This is Jesus, king of the Jews." Below the cross, crowded on the hillside were the people who had come to see Jesus die. Some ran up to the cross and shouted, "Save yourself, come down from that cross, if you are really the Son of God." Others jeered, "What kind of king is this? He saved others, but he cannot save himself. If he is the Messiah, the Christ, let him come down from that cross. Then we will believe him."

The two thieves on either side of Jesus listened to the jeers and insults shouted at Jesus. "Say," remarked one of the thieves, "since you are the Savior, save us."

But the other thief scolded him. "For us, the punishment is fair. We have committed crimes. But this man has done no wrong." The thief turned to Jesus. "Remember me, Lord, when you come into your kingdom," he asked.

Jesus turned his bloodied head to the thief. "Today, you will be with me in Paradise," he told him.

The sky was darkening earlier than usual. The soldiers grouped below the cross played games to pass the time. Lowering his eyes, Jesus saw his followers who had come these last steps to be with him. Among them were John, his beloved apostle, and Mary, Jesus' mother. "Mother, this is your son," he said to Mary and nodded at John. To John, he said, "Son, this is your mother." For Jesus wanted John to take care of Mary.

As the afternoon dragged on, people kept running up to mock Jesus. For hours now, he had hung on the cross. "My God, my God, why have you forsaken me?" he cried out in his agony. It was almost three o'clock. The sky was nearly dark. Jesus leaned back his head. "I thirst," he murmured. Someone ran up with a sponge soaked in sour wine and held it up to his lips.

"It is done," Jesus said, with a loud cry. "Father, into your hands I give my spirit." He bowed his head and died.

308

Darkness spread over the whole land, and the curtain that hung in front of the holy place in the Temple in Jerusalem tore in two, from top to bottom.

"Surely this man was the Son of God," said a soldier standing near the cross.

It was the evening of the Sabbath. Jesus' friends and followers had to bury him immediately, for according to Jewish law, no one was allowed to be buried on the Sabbath day.

Joseph of Arimathea, a rich and important man who was a faithful follower of Jesus, went to Pontius Pilate. Bravely, he asked the Roman governor to let him bury Jesus. Pilate was surprised that Jesus had died so quickly, but he gave his permission. With haste, Joseph returned to Golgotha.

Joseph gently took Jesus' body down from the cross. He wrapped it in fine, clean linen, following the custom of the Jews, and laid it in a new tomb, cut from rock. In front of the tomb, he rolled a heavy stone. Mary Magdelene and Mary, Jesus' mother, watched him close the tomb and then went home to rest on the Sabbath.

# Jesus Comes Back

Darkness edged the sky and
the sun was still rosy when
Mary Magdalene, with some
other women, set out for
Jesus' tomb Sunday morning.
They were bringing spices and
perfumes to clean and preserve
the body.

"Who is going to roll back that heavy stone?" they
wondered as they came to the small garden where the
tomb was located.

Even as they spoke, the stone rolled away. Slowly, the women entered the tomb. To their amazement, the body was gone. While they stood there, afraid and confused, a dazzling figure in the purest white gown appeared.

"Do not be afraid," the angel said. "I know you are

looking for Jesus, but he is no longer here. See, look at the place where he was laid. He has risen from the dead. Go quickly and tell his apostles the news."

In a daze, the women left. Mary Magdalene stood weeping outside the tomb, for she did not really understand what had happened.

"Why are you weeping?" asked a man who was standing behind her.

"Because they have taken away the body of my Lord, and I do not know what they have done with it." Mary thought the man was the gardener. "Please, sir," she asked, "where did you take his body?"

"Mary," the man called. Something in his voice sounded familiar, and Mary turned around. "Master!" she cried, for Jesus was standing by her. She fell to her knees and touched his feet.

"Mary, do not be afraid," Jesus said. "Go to my brothers, and tell them I will see them soon."

Mary's face shone with joy. "I will, my Lord," she said, and went to Jerusalem to tell the apostles.

The apostles did not believe what Mary told them, but John and Peter ran back to the tomb with her. John reached it first. He saw that the stone was rolled back and peered into the tomb. It was empty, except for the linen sheet in which the body of Jesus had been wrapped. Peter was now at the tomb, too. He went inside and saw the linen sheet. Then the two apostles finally understood and believed what Jesus had long ago told them: that he would come back from the dead.

Later that same day two followers of Jesus were going to a village called Emmaus, not far from Jerusalem. As they walked, they talked about everything that had happened. Jesus came to walk with them, but they did not recognize him. "What are you talking about?" he asked. "Why are you so sad?"

"You must be a stranger," answered one man, whose name was Cleopas. "Have you not heard what happened to Jesus of Nazareth? He was a mighty prophet in both words and deeds, but the powerful priests and leaders were afraid of him and handed him over to be killed. We thought Jesus would save the people of Israel. All this happened three days ago. Today some women went to his tomb, and his body was not there. An angel told them he was alive."

"How foolish you are," Jesus said. "How slow you are to believe what has been written about the Messiah by the prophets."

And Jesus walked with them and explained the holy books, beginning with Moses. When they arrived at Emmaus, Jesus looked as if he were going further.

"Stay with us," the men said. "It is late."

They went in together, and Jesus sat down with them at the table. He took the bread, blessed it, and gave each of them a piece. Suddenly, their eyes were opened, and they knew Jesus. But he had vanished. "We should have known it was the Lord," one said. "Did you not feel your heart on fire when he talked with us on the road and explained the holy books to us?"

The two men ran back to Jerusalem. "The Lord has risen. It is true," they told the eleven apostles, who were gathered together for supper. Even as they spoke, Jesus appeared in their midst. The terrified apostles thought they were looking at a ghost.

"Peace be with you," Jesus
said. "Why are you so frightened?
Why do you doubt? Here, look at my
hands, look at my feet. Touch me. A ghost does not have
real flesh and bones.  I have come back to you."

They saw his hands and feet, where they had been
pierced by the soldiers' nails. While the apostles stood
there, torn between joy and doubt, Jesus asked, "Do you
have any food?"

They gave him a piece of broiled fish, and he ate it
as they watched him.

"All this has happened as I said it would. It was
written by the prophets in the Scriptures that I would suffer
and die and rise from the dead on the third day. All these
things you have seen.

"Now you must go into the world and preach this
good news to all the people. Tell them all I have told you.
Those who believe it and follow my words will live forever
in the kingdom of God."

Jesus talked a while with the apostles, then lifted his
hands and blessed all of them.

"I go now to my Father and to your Father, to my God and to your God. But know that I am with you always, until the end of time."

And with these words, Jesus parted from the apostles and was taken up into heaven.